TITAN
WORLD
NOVELLA

DÉJÀ VU

CRISTIN
HARBER

DEJA VU
A TITAN WORLD NOVELLA

Published by Cristin Harber
Copyright © 2017 Cristin Harber

Cover Design and Interior Format

© THE KILLION GROUP INC.

Dear Readers,

Welcome to the Titan World books with stories ranging from military romance to paranormal to contemporary romance. There's something for everyone—action-packed romance, swoon-worthy moments, and happily ever after!

When I started the Titan series, I wanted to combine my love of steamy stories and action-packed suspense. I wrote strong men and women who I hoped readers would fall in love with. I can't think of anything more exciting than opening my world up to very talented authors to extend that experience so that you, the reader, can have a deeper connection to more than one book series at a time.

You will meet new characters and see them interact with familiar ones; you will also see the interpretation of the Titan universe through another author's eyes. I hope that you take the time to experience each book in the Titan World series!

This project was a labor of love. It was a gift for people who believe in #TitanStrong as much as it is someone checking out all the fuss. For every email and message on social media, for every Titan meetup around the globe and empowered post, I know that these books—our books—are more than just romance novels. The characters are our friends when we need a confidante, a hero to save the day when life is just too hard...

I started writing the Titan series about five years ago and never would I have guessed that years later, we would have Team Titan, where I can call you my friends. The books have inspired life goals, tattoos, and relationships. But I believe they have created so much more. You get what you give, and Team Titan is collectively good for the soul.

As for my Titan World contribution, DEJA VU is about a sexy doctor and a CIA spy with amnesia uncovering her past. You've seen Dr. Tuska occasionally in Titan books, but here's a chance to meet the good doc and see how a Titan outsider saves the day with a little help from the team we all know!

Readers, thank you for supporting this project—thank you for believing in me. And, also, thank you for reading and supporting the authors who took time out of their busy writing schedules to participate. The result is amazing.

Titan Hugs and Happy Reading,
Cristin Harber

CHAPTER ONE

THREE STORIES WAS A LONG way to fall onto a frozen ice-slicked sidewalk. That made hanging on to the brick windowsill as sleet pelted against her the only option. "Who comes home early from a honeymoon in an ice storm?"

A better question was why did she choose this window to escape? Seriously, any other window would have been a better choice, but she had chosen the one over a break-her-spine sidewalk. Tragic miscalculation.

Her exhausted muscles screamed for relief. Strength had never been her strong point. Neither had a good manicure, and right now, the pads of her fingertips were probably bleeding as her aching fingers tried to hang on a little while longer. Having pulled herself up once—and God, pull-ups while shivering in the freezing rain were like a task from Satan—she'd seen that the newlyweds were just getting into their... *personal* time. Just a few more minutes, and she could slip back through the window while they were in the throes of distraction and safely escape.

A gust of fierce wind howled. The sleet sliced into her raw cheeks and knuckles as she shivered. Each pelt stung, and her eyelids burned. Watering eyes were the pits, forcing her to blink uncontrollably. There were times instinct served her well. Apparently, there were also times like now.

"The traitors won't win today, damn it." Her teeth chattered as she tried to reposition her frozen fingers on the sill. Everything was numb; she couldn't feel anything. Not her fingers, and not the ledge. Only the frozen pain that was beginning to seep into her bones.

Time for another pull-up. At this point, who cared if the happy love-birds were getting down and dirty? She needed inside.

Harsh gusts of sleet blew from both directions. The near gale-force winds swayed her body. If curiosity killed the cat, what would be said about the CIA agent who died falling out of a journalist's bedroom window?

This house was supposed to be vacant for another day. The reporter wasn't scheduled to come home yet. She'd been lost in his files and paperwork, busy trying to map out intel leaks that were too close to home. She had even briefly seen the name of her boss and Michael Cobin, the secretary of defense.

At least the happy, horny newlyweds had been nice enough to announce their arrival with giggles as they dropped their luggage and groped their way to the bedroom.

Another strong blast of wind almost tore her from the wall. *Damn it!* Agonizingly, she pulled herself up, checking to see if the couple was *very* distracted—thank God! They were under the covers.

She pushed an elbow and her chin up on the windowsill. Her lungs were on fire with the frigid air and exhaustion. Shakily but carefully, she pushed the bottom of the window, sliding it up enough to crawl through. This wouldn't be as graceful as what she'd planned in her head. Her muscles shook. All she needed was enough space to fit through, then to hell with being covert. She would burst in and run like hell through the bedroom. The couple wouldn't know what had happened, and surprise would be on her side, giving her a head start over the two naked people in bed, under the covers. The new plan was as good as it was going to get—

Shit. Her elbow slipped, and her chin scratched down the brick.

Don't fall. Don't fall. The conspiracy theorists would have a field day—if they ever found her body. Which they wouldn't, now that she thought it through. The CIA probably had eyes on her as she dangled, not that they would help her out for going rogue.

She never should have done this. She could have made an appointment. But what would she have said? The truth was nearly *impossible.*

Hot tears slipped free as she struggled to find her grip. Her hand came loose, and she lobbed it numbly above her head. "Get back inside."

She thrust her free hand up, but the other hand came loose. One blissful, euphoric second washed over her in the sleet. Her muscles rejoiced.

No exertion.

No effort.

Pure relaxation.

No! Her brain kicked into action, forcing her cramped hands to reach for the rapidly disappearing windowsill. She fell back in silence, mouth gaping in a nonexistent scream, as she plummeted toward the dark ground.

"It's a whole new world out there." Jared Westin cracked his knuckles as he stood at the front of the small auditorium. He paced and glared around the war-room table at his Titan and Delta teams and at the faces of other elite security teams and his contemporaries. With the hell that the world had seen lately, Titan and a select group of firms had decided that it was in everyone's best interest to summit. Jared had offered their Virginia-based building to host the meetings, and after a few days' worth of operational, tactical, and strategic meetings of the minds, everyone seemed better for it. But... what he hadn't counted on was having to play host by offering his building.

"After this summit, I think we're all comfortable knowing we have each other's backs. If there's anything you get out of these meetings, know that. I've got your six as much as you have mine." Heads nodded. "Small talk isn't my thing, so I'll end this with a simple thanks for coming to Titan. We'll see you out in hell."

Around the room, claps, hurrahs, and thanks broke out from men and women Titan conducted joint operational activities with, along with those from various government and private security firms. But as the meeting adjourned, he watched Beth Hart staring at her phone. Throughout the wrap-up, she'd checked it more than she should have—which was never—and that was out of character.

He walked off the elevated platform. "Hold up, Beth."

She froze and waited while others filed out and down the hall until it was just the two of them.

"Yes, sir?" Beth smiled and gave him the DC socialite presentation the CIA had trained into her and none of the straight shooting he liked.

"Now I know we have a damn problem, Miss Priss." Jared rubbed his face. "Spit it out."

"What?" Her eyes sparkled with a dare.

"Beth, I swear to God, do not make me go fishing into the CIA lake of bull-freaking-shit."

"Company business," she said with a slight lift of her shoulders, giving him the go-get-your-reel response that likely required a bottle of headache medicine and extra paperwork.

"You want to deal with *The Company*, you do it on someone else's time."

"The clock's ticking on this one." She tapped her cell phone. "I didn't have much choice."

Jared didn't care for the CIA's priorities, and sometimes splitting her time with them was more of a hassle than not. "Unless you read me into whatever you're distracted by, I give no shits when they distract you from me. Got it?"

There was her socialite smile again. "You gave a great 'rah-rah, let's be friends' speech. I could glance at my email."

"Now I know you weren't paying attention." He didn't rah-rah cheerlead his own team, much less others. His style of management was much more in the vein of *Get the job done*. For this woman to give him the runaround... *Ah.* She was purposefully testing him. "Explain."

"I don't have anything to explain, Boss Man."

He turned around and pounded boots toward his office. "You better be following me, Beth."

"You already know that I am."

He hid what would've been a smile because she was right. Whatever Beth was about to explain, she was now on record as putting up a fight before he'd worn her down. And that was noteworthy. Beth played games better than almost anyone, and she had just pulled a CYA to deal with a CIA headache because she probably smelled something that stunk.

CHAPTER TWO

ANOTHER DAY, ANOTHER CASE IN which the CIA dropped off a patient with a list of asinine ground rules for James to abide by. If it wasn't one over-the-top thing in the name of national security, it was another. This time, he was to monitor the patient's health and well-being, ensuring that she was medically brought back to life as a *civilian* as quickly and safely as possible. They called her Amnesia Allie. In no uncertain terms was he or his team to assist in recovering her memories. As soon as the spooks had realized one of their own had sustained significant memory loss after an accident, they had *decommissioned the asset*. Meaning, Amnesia Allie no longer worked at the CIA.

James sighed as he flipped his tablet cover closed, shaking his head about how particular the Agency was. Yet so was he. That had likely made their extensive working relationship so successful over the years.

"Hello… *Allie*." James gave his patient in the hospital bed a once-over as she spoke to the nurse. Also hovering nearby, Beth Hart, the CIA's babysitter, and someone he happened to know personally from Jared Westin's Titan Group, stood on guard to monitor Allie.

The nurse barely glanced up from the chart, and Beth acted as though they'd never met. But his patient studied him as if he were the savior who might walk on water. Her stare was altogether unnerving and entrancing. James wasn't sure he'd ever been assessed so quickly, harshly, and intently in his life.

"*That's him.*" Allie's sure voice was directed at him and answered a question from the chart that had been asked before he walked in. Her desperate words held the ragged edge of a plea, which no one else seemed to notice.

The nurse shifted in her plastic-soled shoes, causing them to squeak as Beth sucked a breath of air in surprise so hard she coughed. "You're mistaken, Allie."

Three sets of eyes lay on James so keenly that he could feel them, none stronger than the woman's in the bed. Her gaze *implored*. It was persuasive and convincing, as well as desperate.

"He"—she pushed up on her elbows in the hospital bed—"is my fiancé."

Wait. What did she just say? The nurse gave her a pitying glance, and Beth's eyebrows knotted in annoyance. Apparently, amnesia wasn't supposed to go off script in Beth's world.

The words "I'm not" rested on his tongue, but he stood dumbstruck and locked into a silent conversation with the classic beauty before he tore away and took a nanosecond to consider the spy stuck in bed.

Was she delusional? Imagining that he *was* her fiancé? James chewed his cheek. The nurse wasn't paying any mind, but Beth and Allie were in an all-out silent war for his response. Allie had sent him an SOS without a word, and other than her medical information, all he knew was that she was a CIA asset with amnesia, incorrectly told she had been in a car accident. He had no medical basis on which to make any decision other than to treat the woman and walk away. To do no harm... He had no reason to engage in a discussion, to play to a potential fantasy and put his career on the line.

What did she know that the CIA wanted her to forget? That didn't matter.

It'd been decades since his time in the Army Rangers, but not a day went by in which he didn't see fallout from special operations. Real life had taught him there was a time for the rule book and a time for gut instinct. Right now, his gut instinct fired like an AK-47, so hard and fast that he needed prescription-grade antacid.

James let disbelief wash over his face. "*Allie?*"

"Doctor." If looks could kill, Beth would have just pushed him out the eleventh story window of this hospital room with a hope-it-hurts smile.

He took a step forward, and no one moved. Not Beth, *her friend*, as had been explained to Allie when she woke. Not the nurse, who had busy-bodied in his personal life, or lack thereof, for far too long. And not Allie.

What was he even thinking? He didn't know the decommissioned CIA asset. Yet he had already acknowledged that they had some sort of agreement. "Hi."

Allie's eyes darted to the name embroidered on his white coat. "James."

He fumbled for the next move. "It's been a while…" Playing pretend wasn't his thing. He didn't know what was he doing, but he couldn't stop. Adrenaline spiked in his blood as the cadence of his heartbeat increased.

"It has?" Her confident question went hoarse, and she sounded nearly heartbroken. To any onlooker, it was the raw emotion of two lovers reconnecting. But James knew it for what it was. Raw relief. Terror washing away. His need to protect her grew stronger.

"We aren't engaged any longer," James offered softly, playing to her amnesia that only the two of them knew wasn't a factor.

The nurse gasped at the revelation of the "truth" and this bit of gossip, while Beth's irritation ricocheted off the walls.

Allie's face fell. "We're not?"

He gave a quick nod over his shoulder. "I need the room."

"Doctor," Beth hissed.

He couldn't think. Electricity spiked on his skin as though he were about to jump out the back of a chopper into the inky black night. Having no idea how the next moments would go exhilarated him as much as it made him hungry to get to know Allie.

Consciously, James took a deep breath to slow his heart rate. "I'd like to speak with my patient privately, and I think Allie would like a familiar face at a time like this."

Beth stepped closer to the bed. "Allie, I can stay."

"I'm fine." She tucked the blankets around her legs on the bed and stared as the nurse slowly made her way to the door.

"We have catching up to do." He sliced Beth with a stare that was all but an order. If she wanted to play the good friend, she could step out. But if she wanted to wear the CIA's hat and not leave them alone, then Beth could have that conversation right now, but they both knew that wouldn't happen.

"All right, Allie. We have a lot to catch up on from what you *do* remember." Beth pasted on her socialite charm and acted the role of the caring friend. "I'll be right out in the hall if you need anything."

Allie didn't respond, having buttoned up a layer of invisible armor. Her eyes locked onto him just as Beth's had. Two sets of stares, both with very different meanings. There would be hell to pay for this breach in the CIA's script, but sometimes, even the strict doc needed to go with the flow.

He hadn't built a niche, concierge medical practice overnight that catered to the types of *special* requests he received from the CIA, to be bossed around on a pointless job.

Beth shifted her weight in her high heels, pivoting so that she could take them both in. "Allie, I'm your friend." She took a step closer. "He's your doctor."

"Again, I'm fine," Allie insisted and pushed back in her bed.

Beth didn't budge, and he didn't expect her to. A bullish white-knight urge came over him, and he wanted to protect Allie from Beth.

"Allie—" Beth tried again.

She put her hand up as if to physically block the word away from her. "I don't know you."

Beth's bold smile flickered. "Honey, we're friends. I know you don't remember anything." She faux-hesitated. "I was listed as your emergency contact. Don't you think that means something?"

"Beth, is it?" James threw a stare that could have knocked over an armored vehicle. "Why don't you give us a minute? I promise she'll be fine."

The war was on as to who would give in first.

"Sure thing, Doc." Beth waved the white flag, and then her expensive heels clacked on the tile until he and Allie were all alone.

Shit, he would hear about this later. But that didn't matter. Beth slammed the door shut right after the nurse skittered out, and he shifted back to his patient, or his... ex-fiancée. "Allie."

"Doctor, I'm—"

"If we were engaged, it's James." He tapped his lab coat, where she had read his name before.

She blushed, and he couldn't help but smile at the innocent way it tinged her cheeks. "*James.*"

"Nice to meet you," he said, letting that unhidden smile find his words.

"Likewise." She shifted on the bed. "About that, though..."

He waited expectantly in an easy silence.

"Actually"—Allie tugged her bottom lip between her teeth—"I wish I had a good reason for pulling that out of nowhere."

"That?" James pushed.

"I called you my fiancé." She blushed again, giving her fair skin a work-out.

"I said you were." Between her light-brown hair and eyes, and the third, maybe fourth time she had blushed around him, James found her... entrancing. Perhaps he was crazy too. She was in a hospital gown and very clearly had days-old eye makeup that was smudged and semi-wiped away, but not removed. No one ever looked great staying in a hospital room for more than a day, yet Allie did. Her chin was scabbed, her cheeks had signs of windburn, and still she could've turned heads.

She sighed as though her charade was up. "Now you're going to mark up that I'm nutzo."

"Are you?" He shoved his hands in his coat jacket and ignored the urge to sit next to her.

"No."

"Now that we've cleared that up…" Still, he couldn't stay away. Hands in the pockets wasn't enough of a barrier, and James stepped closer to her bed. "Any questions for me?"

"Why did you agree? That you were my ex-fiancé?"

Good question. He took a deep breath and held it before letting it drift out. "Call it instinct."

"Instinct…" She toyed with her hospital gown, smoothing it and focusing on a loose string. "Hmm."

James pulled his hands out and crossed his arms, deciding to push. "Hmm?"

"Thank you for taking a chance."

"I'll take your non-answer for now if you tell me why you needed a fiancé?"

"I didn't need a fiancé." Eyes defensive, she lifted her shoulder but winced. "I just needed someone on my side and knew it could be you."

"You're in pain?" He reached for his tablet and swiped the screen awake, quickly bringing up her chart. She'd turned away pain meds?

"I'm not taking anything that could make me feel fuzzy."

Not even simple painkillers. The CIA and their games produced trust issues even when one wasn't aware of their involvement in their own life. He didn't blame Allie at all. What did she know about the CIA, though? "You have Beth. She's a friend who can help."

"So she says."

"How much of your memory is actually gone?" he asked. She was so close to the truth that he had to wonder if it was all a game.

Her face fell. "All of my memory is gone; I just have a feeling—you have instincts, I have a feeling. I know what Beth has told me, and I needed a neutral safe harbor. You don't know me. You don't know her. You're Switzerland."

Well, shit. Their fake ex-engagement was starting on a lie and he already hurt the girl's feelings. Man, he was screwing this relationship up already.

But more than that, James was impressed that, without a memory, she could pick out a mole in the room and see Beth for what she was. Not one to be trusted.

Allie dropped her chin. "See? It sounds crazy. But I don't feel like she's my friend. I don't feel like I'm anything she's told me about *me*."

He couldn't imagine how frustrating that had to be. He was contracted to not say a word. To walk out the door as quickly as he came in. But not helping her when she was clearly grasping at straws of her former self was nearly medical malpractice and ethically bankrupt. That, and it was a total dick move. "Who do you think you are, Allie?"

"*Not* an introvert, work-from-home Internet marketer." She made a face, twisting her mouth and rolling her eyes.

He burst out laughing. "That's what she said you were?"

"Yes." Allie deepened her smirk now that they were both in on the joke. "You don't believe it, either."

He tilted his head. "I wonder how we would've met."

"What do you mean?"

"Since you were an introvert who worked from home."

"Oh." Allie laughed, relaxing in a thought. "Maybe at the grocery store or a gas station?" She tugged the neck of her hospital gown. "Maybe after a fender bender gone wrong or something?"

"Or something." Maybe they'd paired up on a CIA operation in which the Agency had needed him out in the field on an op. Or that was just his fantasy...

She pulled her hair off her shoulders as though she were going to pull it into a ponytail and winced. "Odd place for a bump from a car accident."

Nope. Allie didn't just fall off the turnip truck. The hospital room door opened, and Beth powered in, woman on a mission to stop the nefarious relationship-history building. Now *he* was the one who was going to get pissed because fake ex or not, Allie was a breath of fresh air in his normal ho-hum day. Beth could cool her heels already.

"We weren't done yet," Allie snapped before he could.

James sidestepped in front of Beth and intercepted her play. Careful not to show they knew one another, he dropped his voice low. "Easy. You're treading on my turf."

Beth's lipsticked mouth pressed into a tight line. Her polished gaze swept between them, ignoring the nurse who reappeared at the door.

"Allie." James pivoted to have both women in his view. "Beth understands we weren't done yet. She'll give us the room again. She's worried, and that just makes her a good friend."

One second, then another tick of time passed before Beth surrendered. "Sure thing, Doc. I'll be back later."

The door slammed again, almost on the nurse this time.

"She was kind of mad," Allie whispered.

"Yup." There would be Hell. To. Pay.

CHAPTER THREE

BETH STORMED INTO JAMES'S PRIVATE office, and the glass door hit the wall, making his diplomas and awards jump. He tossed down his pen, and the heavy weight of the Montblanc hit his desk with a thud then rolled once until a gold lapel pin stopped it in place.

He stared at the expensive black pen instead of her, cracked his neck once, and pushed back in his leather chair. "Well, hello to you too."

Beth put her hands on her hips. "You were never her fiancé! What are you doing?"

"Who is she really? And don't give me some BS-filled résumé that the CIA put together, because frankly, I've already read it. Whoever she worked with before isn't here. And it wasn't you."

"Damn it, James!"

He bounced back in his chair twice, assessing Beth. The woman was fit to be tied and that said volumes. The more she pushed, the more he'd buckle down on his move. "How do you know we weren't engaged before? You don't. We were. End of story."

"You sound like a petulant two-year-old. It's a matter of national security."

He crossed his arms at that song and dance. "You have no idea what it's a matter of. You're following orders."

"So should you," Beth shot back.

"I will remind you"—he leaned forward—"I have no orders to follow. I don't work for anyone but my patients, and you know that."

Exasperation rolled off her. When Beth worked, she was cool as a cucumber straight out of the crisper, but when she had the chance to vent, her temper could fly. She paced back and forth in front of his desk.

"You know, the people who pace in front of my desk are generally making life-and-death decisions. They have far more weighty decisions on their minds than trying to handle the backstory of an amnesia patient."

Beth threw her arms out. "You were never engaged."

"The love of my life broke my heart long ago. I have done nothing to interfere with whatever it is you're doing. And I have listened to everything the CIA has asked of me, despite how questionable this one seems to be."

Beth glowered, and her flawless makeup didn't hide her disdain as she stalked to the front of his desk, her fists balled. "You don't know what you're messing with, Doc."

James shook his head. "I suspect, Beth, that you don't either. And if that is all, you can storm out."

CHAPTER FOUR

L ONDON. PARIS. NEW YORK CITY. Those weren't the places James wanted to be. When Allie was in his office, the place had a different energy. Having her visit him gave his day an extra lift, and he didn't feel as though they were sitting in Summerland Hospital's row of offices. It honestly didn't matter where they were.

Today was different, though. Between their conversation about her health and discharge papers, the mood was darker... though neither of them had said as much.

"I'm sorry." Allie rubbed her temples, letting her soft-looking hair fall over her face. "It's just I have this sense of déjà vu, and it's been driving me crazy."

"It's—"

"I know that's part of recovery."

James rolled a Montblanc pen between his fingers, its weight seemingly garnering far more of his interest than what was needed. "You should talk to your specialist about that."

What a stupid answer. He hated to give her that answer, but he had no choice.

"You're not even curious what's causing it?" Her analytical eyes bored into him, and he didn't even need to look up to know her assessment was in full swing.

That wasn't déjà vu; it was her survival instinct. James pressed his lips together and raised his brows. He had nothing to say, nothing he *could* say, so he played with his pen.

Allie's unexpectedly powerful hand slapped on top of his. "Why is everybody lying to me?"

Her palm was hot, her fingers strong as they gripped the tops of his and squeezed. He tugged his hand back, and she ripped his hand forward.

"Dr. Tuska—"

"*James.*" *Damn it.* She needed to let go, because he didn't want to. He hated lying to her, hated when she referred to him as her doctor, hated when she didn't say his name. Because he wanted to hear her say James! And to kiss her. So hell, she needed to let go! Now!

Allie's eyes narrowed. "James, I don't understand why you listen to everything I have to say except for when I talk about me!"

He snatched his hand away, breathing harder than he should have been. Hell, turned on when he never should have been at all. "It's an injury, and there's a recovery process."

She stared at the ceiling. "That's not at all what I'm talking about, and you know it. Beth knows it. Everybody who I talk to knows it." She dropped her gaze, thankfully appearing to have missed the last thirty seconds of his thoughts and reactions to her. "I feel like they're rewriting my history, and I don't understand why."

"I don't understand, either," he admitted, focusing on the real issue.

They sat in silence, avoiding why she was there—to say good-bye after she was given her discharge papers. "Beth is going to take me home. And I was going to order pizza. Do you want to join us— Shoot, that sounds like a date. I wasn't asking you on a date. I'm sorry. It's just... I don't know anybody. Or the people that everybody says that I do know, I don't know." She looked away.

Before he needed to kiss her. Touch her. Now all he wanted to do was offer her a hug and tell her it would be okay. "It didn't sound like a date. No worries." Though if it had, he would have said yes. What were the rules on asking out a patient who was supposedly an ex? That could be done. Not that complicated. The problem was that her connection to the CIA made her off limits.

"Knock, knock, I'm here," Beth said as she appeared at the door. "How's everybody doing?"

Allie turned in her chair and put on a fake smile. "I guess I'm doing okay."

Even Beth's cheery disposition didn't lift the fog from the room. James settled back as Beth did her best to entertain her friend.

The whole faux show hurt to watch. But this was his job, and it wasn't the first time he'd seen the CIA's bullshit. Though it was the first time James had cared.

CHAPTER FIVE

THE DOORBELL RANG IN THE foreign house, and Allie jumped, nearly choking on her pizza. It was her fifth slice of the night. The first two she'd eaten with Beth. The second two she'd had alone. And this fifth piece she was having with a bottle of wine—well, at least the start of a bottle of wine. Two glasses in and two bites deep, she quickly dabbed at her mouth and walked to her door, wondering who on earth would be knocking.

It was far too late for any mail delivery, and as it turned out, she apparently didn't have a lot of friends. She worked online, where people knew her, and she belonged to mega marketing groups. Everybody was familiar with her profiles.

But as for real live people? Apparently, Allie didn't have those.

Warily, she stared at the door as the doorbell rang again. "Coming."

Anxiety at the unknown door knocker struck, and her hands felt empty, as though she should have been running them along her hips, searching for something. She glided against the wall and checked outside as best she could without being seen.

James.

James stood on the front porch as though the soles of his shoes had been glued to Allie's doormat and gaped. At home in sweatpants and a T-shirt, Allie had her hair thrown into a ponytail. She was gorgeous just like that as she stood there, holding the front door open. His mind flashed back to the night she'd arrived at Summerland Hospital. Even though she had just been through a trauma, he'd known this was what his idea of beauty and the future looked like. This woman at home.

Shit. What was he doing there?

"I didn't expect you." Allie's wide eyes showed the interest that she couldn't understand and didn't trust, and *that* he knew all too well.

"I wanted to check on you and should've called." His landlocked stance loosened, and he took a bold step forward despite her lack of invitation. "But there was the chance you'd say no. You weren't clear on your interest in a date."

Her eyes went wide. "*A date?*"

He needed to backtrack. "Not a date. Just checking on a woman who told the world she was my ex-fiancée for a solid week."

Truth was, now that she had left the hospital, he missed stopping by her room before he left for the night, and he'd missed her in his office the moment she waved good-bye. They had messed with the nurses, screwed with Beth, had laughs, shared a few stories, and caught up on a life they hadn't had together. They'd become fast friends over a relationship that hadn't existed. There were sparks for him. Did she feel them too? He had to know, and tonight, he couldn't stay away. Was he more than just her security blanket?

He wanted to be, and he had no idea how that was possible. She'd used him as a life raft in an uncertain week as she questioned everything else, except for the one certain lie that she told as a truth: *them.*

"I'm fine. Nothing a little bit of pizza couldn't cure." Allie bit her lip. "And... I wouldn't have said no to a date." She took a rushed step back, shyness brightening her cheeks. "But—"

He caught her hand. It was soft and delicate, fitting nicely in his. The first time they had touched outside the confines of Summerland Hospital, and his pulse jumped as her face shot up. "Allie, hey."

"Hey."

His thumb swiped across her knuckles. "It's good to see you."

Her eyelashes fluttered. "It's only been a few hours."

"I don't care."

A pretty pink lit her cheeks under the glow of her porch light. "Would you like to come in?"

That was why he was here, wasn't it, after all? He squeezed her hand. Everything about this would have been perfect if he'd never lied to her. "I'd like to."

Nervously, Allie took her hand back and swept her arm into the room. "Welcome to the house that I don't remember. It doesn't feel like mine. *Mi casa es su casa.*"

Was it even her home? James wanted to trigger a memory of what might have been here before and what had been removed by the CIA cleanup team. But first, he had to get through the door. "Maybe it'll feel more like home after a day or two."

She sidestepped the well-decorated hallway. "You sound like you believe that as much as I do."

The entryway was clear of anything out of place. No tossed jacket, no kicked-off pile of shoes. He tended to be a neat freak, but when an unexpected guest walked into his home, they could tell he lived there. Not like this place. It was far too clean. James would have bet money that she hadn't lived there before.

Allie led the way to a dining room table, where a piece of pizza and a bottle of wine waited.

"I'll get you a glass," she offered.

"I'm good." She shouldn't have been drinking. He glanced around at the house that could have been picture ready for a house accessories catalogue photo shoot. Nothing was out of place. Even the pile of junk mail on a side table looked expertly placed. He leaned over to spy... Just as he'd thought. The address labels had her name laser printed on. It was too much. Since when did junk mail come addressed by name instead of "Our Friends" or "The Neighborhood Household"? Maybe one or two pieces, but not a pile of crap she would likely toss. It'd been staged.

"If you're here, you're going to have to drink." She left him to his inspection as she padded away to get a glass from the dining room hutch.

"Really. I'm fine."

Having returned, she held his glass to her chest as if she were guarding it against what he might say next. "I'm not drinking by myself when you're here, and I don't want to ignore my wine. You have two options: leave or have a glass of wine."

"You shouldn't even be drinking right now." He stalled. Alcohol would lessen his ability to think clearly around her, and with this woman, he needed all his faculties. "Doctor's orders. You know that."

"I know there's a choice on the table, Doctor."

But all he could think about was the swell of her breasts as she held the glass. "Allie—"

"I can't remember. I hate this. I just, I don't know." She dropped her head and let the wine glass slip away from her chest and dangle haphazardly in her hand. "Sorry. You must think I'm crazy. Once again."

Her pedicured toes wiggled as she stared hopelessly at them. To reach for memories while in recovery, only to be told they weren't true when in fact they were, was a true mind fuck. Very much the style of the CIA.

He stepped closer, partially drawn by the light scent of her perfume and partially by the need to help her. The damn doctor in him wanted to alleviate her pain. How screwed up was that when he knew more than he could share, and it was destroying her? "I'll have a glass."

Her face perked up. "Good answer."

Allie poured his glass and topped hers off.

"Join me on the couch?" he asked, eyeing the wraparound living room.

She laughed. "Seems like I should invite you. They're my couches and all."

"*Are they?*" He teased, and her mood lifted back to where it had been. "Come on." He took both their glasses as they made their way to the couch as if they were old friends.

She threw herself onto the overstuffed leather couch and, a minute later, rubbed her face. "I needed to laugh. I felt like me for a second. I do when you're near me."

"Happy to help." That was like saying he was okay with breathing. There wasn't another place he would rather be.

CHAPTER SIX

JAMES LET THE REALIZATION OF how deep he might be for a woman he hadn't kissed sink in. She was CIA trained. Maybe he had made a miscalculation along the way—

Allie gulped two big sips. "When did we get engaged?"

"Whoa, Allie," James said. "I am positive your brain trauma specialist told you that alcohol wasn't a great idea to begin with. But sloshing it down like that? *Not a great idea.*"

She gave him the side eye over the brim of her wine glass. "Did you come over here to be my doctor?"

Not at all. "But I *am* a doctor."

"So, you must say something?" she asked, teasing him with a pretend sip of wine.

He nodded, feeling the warmth of her playfulness hit him. This had nothing to do with her being CIA trained; Allie was giving him the real deal. One hundred percent honesty. Which was more than he could say about himself at the moment.

"Do you always have to tell the truth to your patients?"

"Sure—"

"You know something more than you're letting on. Right?"

Shit. Walked into that one. "Allie—"

"Why don't you start by telling me what nobody wants to tell me?" She pressed her lips into a thin, flat line that reminded him of a flatline on an electrocardiogram. This conversation needed to die. "Because I know I sound like an insane crazy person. I know I *sound* delusional. But I also know that I'm *not.* Because if I was, I'd probably be locked up somewhere. I would have a medical history full of mental illness. But I don't. And I know that someone like you wouldn't have said we were engaged."

Or he could resuscitate the conversation by changing directions. "Like me, how?"

She went for a sip of wine but turned her head at the last moment and set her glass on the coffee table. "Perfect. Organized. I bet your house might even look like this. Like you walked out on a regular day, when you didn't expect anyone to see it, and it was pristine."

"It's not."

She raised a judging eyebrow. "Really?"

"Well..." He took a seat on the other side of the couch. "Everything has a place."

"Even the random, unorganized crap looks placed there on purpose."

"You're analyzing the hell out of little details."

Both of her eyebrows arched high as though they wanted to jump off her forehead and shake him for being intentionally obtuse. "Wouldn't you, if memories were just a fingertip's distance away, yet..."

Yes, he would. "I'm not sure."

"Bullshit, James. And you know it."

"Allie—"

"My calendar goes back three years, and it's perfect. Perfect! No mistakes. No errors. No missed appointments. My emails? They're so boring! The small talk in them is enough to make somebody lose their mind. I didn't write that. Nobody would write that. Who was I talking to? Who are these people that I was conversing with? There's no style. There's no voice. It sounds like somebody wrote emails to themselves back and forth, back and forth, back and forth, and then put them in my email box. It's a patchwork of perfect names, a correct proportion of female-to-male conversations, a joke over the course of a few years. But it's mass-produced junk. Filler."

"Well... maybe the new you is more... hungry for different experiences?"

Allie mouthed O-M-G. "I'm a marketing person who never left my house. I had online conversations and apparently one friend. Beth. Her emails don't even sound like her."

That sounded as though some entry-level CIA desk jockey had typed out three years of correspondence for a marketing person and then made a fake email history. She might've forgotten her life, and the Farm boys might have been working on an extraordinarily tight deadline, but Allie wasn't stupid. Why hadn't they killed her?

"I'm going to figure it out," Allie whispered as though he wasn't meant to hear.

He contained his uneasy grimace. Not that he didn't want her investigating, but he genuinely was concerned for her life if she did.

"Maybe you just work with boring people." He burrowed deep against the comfortable couch.

"My Internet history is ridiculous. It's strictly work, a few recipes, and the weather."

He shrugged. "I don't see the problem."

"Exactly. That's the problem. Everything is so clean. So perfect. Have you ever heard that unsaid rule—or maybe it's just something said between girlfriends. Except I apparently have none other than Beth—that if I die, go to my house and go find my vibrator and clean out my browser history before my mom does? It's the job of a best friend."

Awkwardness and red-hot heat crawled up his neck. "Maybe Beth did that?"

Allie grinned, maybe noticing that she put him in the world's most uncomfortable of places, seeing as he wanted to be a damn gentleman. "I'm being serious. *There isn't even a vibrator here!*"

Alright already! A thousand inappropriate thoughts sent fire blazing and getting an erection wouldn't be a smart move, but holy hell. "But—"

"Pull up your Google history." She reached for his phone. "Tell me what the last things were you asked Siri about."

James batted her hand away. "Patient confidentiality."

That and he didn't know what he'd been searching or Googling for the last few weeks. He couldn't remember the last few things he had asked Siri, but he probably wanted to review it before he showed Allie.

"See?" She inched forward, motioning to his phone. "You could show me non-work things, but you're hesitating."

"All right, point made. Not that there's anything questionable on my phone. But I understand what you're saying."

She settled back against the couch and reached for the wine but apparently decided against it. "I can dig down three levels"—she threw her hands in the air—"and then that's it."

It wasn't fair that he could partake and she couldn't, but hell. Vibrators—2, James—0. He took a hearty drink of his wine.

The old Allie was scratching at the surface, roaring to get out. Nobody except a trained operative would have pulled those things together, especially while in recovery. It was just that simple.

He put down his glass. "What is it that you need from me? Besides the information that you think I have. What can I do to make any of this better?"

Allie stared at him, and the seconds felt like centuries. "I have no idea."

His heart shattered. She could grasp the straws but didn't know how to make the connections.

"If this was my boring, sucky life"—she tilted her head around the room despondently—"maybe I should try to get used to it."

"Allie." His throat ached. So did his heart.

Finally, her searching gaze stopped on the television. "Do you want to watch a movie with me? *Ex*-fiancé and all, but I'd like somebody to lean against and watch a movie with. No more doctor-patient weirdness, right?"

There was her blush again. The strong operative transformed into the cute woman when she made a move. She could talk about sex toys without batting an eyelash, but inviting him for a movie was almost too much. Too bad there was a reason he should say no: he was lying to her about everything.

CHAPTER SEVEN

WHY DID A MOVIE SOUND like crossing a line when so many had been crossed already? Leaving would have been best, maybe for both of them. Because for how attracted he was to her and how much he wanted to care for her, help her… *he couldn't.* James never made time for relationships, yet here he was. He'd made a leap of faith for Allie and put his licensure at risk along with his standing with the Agency. He didn't want to leave at all.

"Or you can go." Allie laughed with a downplaying grin. "I'll even pack you some cold pizza for the road."

He wasn't going anywhere. "A movie works. See if one piques your interest, and maybe it will help with your memory." Or not… The unsolicited advice came out automatically. He needed to shut up any time now.

Her face fell. "Thought you weren't here as my doctor."

"I'm not." James ran his hand along her arm and watched goose bumps pop up. "Go pick a movie."

"Right," Allie whispered. "Maybe a movie will help my memory."

"How about this? I'll find something in the movie to relate to me. Silly first date talk. That way, it's nothing like doctor's orders. Deal?"

"Deal."

She pushed off the couch, and he let his fingers drift over her as she pulled away. Allie walked to the wall and pulled open a shelf, running her finger along DVD jackets. "Rom-com. Comedy." She shook her head. "I feel like I would totally be into some action-adventure movies. I feel like that would be me." She turned. "Would my taste in movies be forgotten?"

Not really… "Thought I wasn't here as your doctor tonight."

"Oh, brother. Walked into that one." She turned back and grabbed a movie. "Comedy it is. I won't torture you with anything too romantic. I feel like I've tortured you enough."

The woman had no idea. The torture was just beginning. Having her curled up next to him for the duration of a movie would be tough. Pseudo first date or not, he was still a gentleman. Even if he had to keep repeating mental reminders.

Allie grabbed a blanket and took a seat next to James, doing the agonizing thing of sitting far too close to him—and she smelled like an angel. Like vanilla. Allie, the angel. Shit, he was losing his mind. The two of them could be mindless together.

G

Allie couldn't breathe when James tossed his arm over the back of the couch. God, it was too much to take, but he was not nearly close enough. She loved the high-flying feeling of raw attraction. A shiver burst over her skin at the memory, or actually lack thereof. She'd never felt like this before—of that, she was certain.

"What should I expect? Meg Ryan?" He settled back and relaxed while she pressed Play and pulled the blanket over her lap, building a line of demarcation. If they didn't cross it, there would be no problems. She'd apparently not had enough wine before he arrived to brave moving an inch closer.

"I promised no rom-com. Have no worries."

James smelled shower-fresh, unlike the scrubbed-doctor scent from the hospital. Oh God, not that she'd been smelling him.

His chuckle burst out. "Okay, I didn't expect to really laugh at this."

She'd totally missed it! Lost in her head about—

"Come here." He dropped his arm around her shoulders and ignored the blanket fortress she'd built. "Get out of your head."

"I'm not in my head." But the protest was an obvious lie.

"Allie." His voice dropped low, and she let him tug her under his arm, snuggling her into place against his side. "If you're not going to watch the movie, what is it that you want?"

"I can't tell you," she whispered.

A funny exchange happened in the movie, but this time, he didn't laugh. His eyes were focused on her, and his arm around her shoulders made her heart slam against her ribcage.

"You didn't laugh this time," she pointed out.

"Wasn't paying attention to the movie," he said.

Oh God. With her heartbeat on speed, now her lungs had declared war on breathing. "Maybe the movie was a bad idea."

He dropped his head close to hers. The warmth of his lips brushed against hers. Her mouth watered for his kiss, and her body liquefied. Begging would be poor form, but the anticipation might be her death. "Please" was about to form as a pout on her lips, when James let their distance evaporate.

Ah, the fireworks. Her pliant lips molded to his as he slipped his tongue into her mouth, teasing a moan from the depths of her. Her lungs had kick-started back to work, but she couldn't get enough oxygen to avoid the lightheadedness. Wet between her legs, nipples aching for his touch, Allie was drunk on him, and that was just a first kiss. Just the best kiss of her life. She didn't care that she couldn't remember another man. Some things, she just knew.

He groaned. His arm became a vise, wrapping around her shoulders. James shifted her onto his thigh. A heat broke out across her skin, a deep awareness that this was one of those kisses that ended in orgasms.

Allie wanted him inside her. She wanted her breasts in his hands and his tongue in her mouth as she came on his cock. Her hungry hands found his shirt, tugging it, needing him desperately.

"Wait." James gasped and grabbed her arm. "I don't know that you should do that, Allie."

"You don't want me?" she pressed, knowing he felt everything she did. Whatever her previous life was, she knew she could read people. And what she could read loud and clear between them was red-hot chemistry.

"Maybe you need time." The pained expression on his face didn't lessen the fact that she could feel his erection. "We should slow down."

She tightened her fingers into a hell-no grip on his shirt, letting them scratch his abdomen muscles in the process. James's hungry eyes dropped.

Allie whispered against his cheek. "I'm sick of everyone telling me what's best for me. If you don't want me, then say that." Because being under his arm like this was like a memory she wanted to have but hadn't experienced yet. Everything was as it should have been, and she couldn't explain it. "But I need you."

James ran his strong fingers along her back, and every inch of her skin rejoiced. His other hand cupped her cheek, his thumb drifting over her flesh as if he were savoring the experience. If he didn't kiss her again, didn't take her to bed, her tears would fall again, and—

James stole her breath with a sweet kiss. "Such an angel."

He feathered another kiss that went straight to her heart, which made no sense, but she didn't care. Every moment since she'd woken, she'd had to be strong. But right now? She could be as fragile as an eggshell, and he would take care of her.

"James…" Everything she needed was in the breath of that kiss. Maybe they had been lovers in another life, because the earthquake of a man holding her close rocked her world before they'd even made love.

His warm breath sent her into a mind-melding abyss. "Yes?"

"We're on the same page?" Her words were intermixed with deep kisses.

James slipped his palms under her sweatshirt in an answer, and as his skin made contact with her waist, she knew they weren't getting off that couch… at least not anytime soon.

"Good." Shrugging out of the sweatshirt for him, she let it fall to the ground.

"You're beautiful, angel." He laid her on the couch, catching her off guard.

With James over top of her, she lost her thought. Her mind had been such a traitorous bitch.

"You're the only one I believe."

Feeling guilty, James shifted his gaze. "Allie…"

"Please look at me."

He brought his face back. "Angel, there's something in your past, and neither of us knows exactly what it is."

She wanted to cry but wouldn't waste their moment. "I trust your kisses and believe in your smiles. The only thing I want is for you to make love to me."

With a look that was as solemn as a vow, James slowly stripped off her sweatpants and unfastened her bra until she lay under him in only her panties.

He stripped away his shirt, displaying toned muscles. His biceps were heavy and matched strong forearms. Her healing fingertips touched his chest hair as James worked down her neck, kissing softly and letting his hands explore her swollen breasts as she melted under him. He paid attention to the slope of her collarbone, whispering how she tasted as heavenly as she smelled.

Allie's insides swirled, and her mind spun. When he sucked her nipple into his mouth, the wet heat spiked her higher than the clouds. James had her soaring. He had her carefully pinned beneath him, and she was more aroused, more turned on than she knew she could be. This close to him, she could see the tiniest flecks of gray in his light-brown hair, and she feathered kisses along the top of his head, pressing her lips to his thick hair and anything else she could find contact with—until his fingers went between her legs. At that moment, the dizzying sensation struck her stupid. Allie could do nothing but toss her head back and close her eyes.

"Good, angel?" James asked, dancing his fingers over her wet folds. He teased her clit and brushed his knuckles over her sensitive skin, encouraging her to open for him.

"Yes. *Very* good."

For as harsh and hot as her thoughts about him had been, he was going slowly and making this so right.

James slipped off the couch, dropping to the side and snagging off her underwear, and repositioned her with a swift move. For all his preparation to ease his way there, he didn't hold back now.

"God, James," Allie cried as he rolled his eager tongue over her clitoris before sucking it between his lips.

"Mmm."

He held her eyes, the vibrations from his voice running up her spine and down her arms.

She gripped the blanket and gasped as he eased down, dropping to kiss her entrance. The start of his five o'clock shadow had gone unnoticed until now, and the light scratch was cataclysmic. "Oh…"

He licked, stroking her deeper, until his tongue had worked its way inside her, and she couldn't breathe.

"Please," she gasped. Her emotions and hormones were overwhelming her, and she was drunk on the need to come. "James. This is so unreal. God. But please…" She pulled her hips back. "Wait."

Confused, he paused. "What?"

Panting, she couldn't stand a separation between them, couldn't handle this moment lacking specialness despite their rush. "The first time I come with you, please, *please* be inside me."

He blinked as though not understanding.

"*James*, I am dying. Please."

"Killing me, Allie." He moved her back and stood, unfastening his pants and stepping out of them. She watched him remove the condom from his wallet and roll it on. James was meticulous in all things; how purposefully he made love shouldn't shock her. Yet as he descended upon her, she was overcome by just how all-consuming he was.

With his mouth against her neck, his hand guided his thick shaft back to where his mouth had been. Allie moaned as he pressed into her body. He nuzzled her cheek and kissed her lips, keeping his eyes open as hers were. Their eyes locked. James thrust, and her jaw clenched. This was what she needed, slow and steady, drowning her in pleasure.

"There you go," he crooned.

She flexed her hips to meet him, and their kisses tangled. Her climax built quickly, and why it was important that he feel it too, she would never know. But hell... "I'm going to—"

James gave her what she needed, stroking deep, holding her close.

She came, and as he clung to her, he came too. She couldn't stop kissing him. Their breaths seesawed back and forth. Panting gasps from the highest mountain began to slow as they held each other and floated down. Maybe this was why she'd needed to come with him. Who knew, but it was perfect.

"Stay with me tonight?" she whispered against his cheek.

James didn't respond. He didn't have to. She knew. Wordlessly, they went down a hall and got into her bed. Before she could process that maybe everything happened for a reason and that her old life wasn't worth searching for, James had her tucked to his side in a bed she didn't know. He pulled her close to his chest and tucked the comforter around her exhausted, sated body. "Go to sleep, angel."

The man was more familiar than her covers, and she breathed deeply before giving in to sleep.

CHAPTER EIGHT

ALLIE ROLLED OVER AND CAUGHT James's scent on her pillow. That was not how she had expected last night to go, and with her shower running in the background and her sheets sleep rumpled, she could still feel how they'd spent the night on the couch before going to bed.

"It was perfect," she whispered. Then her eyes drifted shut as she fell into the easy slumber of a morning afterglow.

The tickle of a familiar memory pulled at her subconscious. Allie squeezed her eyes tighter. Surely, this was something she had done in the past—had sex, hello. But the strike of the feeling, *the emotion*, struck her in a way that made her want to physically reach for the memory and tuck it under the covers with her.

Water splashed in the adjacent bathroom, and Allie recalled a memory with such force that it knocked the breath out of her. People kissing. So close that she had to run and hide. A balcony? A window? It was cold. So cold and wet. But not last night, and not in her house.

She struggled to look around, but the memory wouldn't allow it. She wanted to open her eyes but didn't dare. She was awake, yet this was a dream. Then it was gone!

Allie sat up in bed, panting, desperate to find that thought again, but she couldn't see it and couldn't place it. The feeling was still with her, though. The water turned off, and she turned and stared at the bathroom. Who had she seen kissing? Why had she run away? Did she have a real ex-fiancé?

Allie jumped out of bed and ran to her dresser, dressing as quickly as she could. She didn't know what she was doing; she just needed to find out the answers, and she wasn't going to do that naked. After a quick pull of underwear, she snapped on a bra and yanked on a hoodie. Allie grabbed socks and pulled on sweatpants. The bathroom door opened, and she spun. James had shower-wet hair and a towel around his waist. He looked wet and warm and like somebody she needed to trust right now.

"I remembered something. But I didn't. I felt it. But it was something." Her hands tore into her messy hair. "God! What is wrong with me?"

"*Nothing*, Allie." He rushed over, attempting to hold her, but she couldn't handle being restrained.

"It was more than just a memory. Why can't I remember anything, and why do I feel like I should remember everything?"

"That's part of the frustration—"

"No!" She warily looked down at her body, the one James had kissed and loved on last night, the one she had spent time studying alone in quiet. What she was about to say would mark her as crazy all over again. "I wasn't in a car accident. I don't believe it. I was hit hard enough to lose my memory, and my body aches, but in all the wrong places. My *hands* hurt so badly when I came to. And have you seen my fingernails? The tips of my fingers? They are *ragged*."

He shifted awkwardly. "Then get a manicure."

"James!" Tension closed her throat as if the noose that had been constricting around it had finally yanked tight.

"Look—if you saw how you ran off the road…" He trailed off unconvincingly.

"Do you know? That it wasn't a car accident?"

James shook his head. "No, Allie." But he stopped himself before defending the absurd accident anymore.

She didn't have bruises from a seat belt. "Just now, I remembered watching someone. I was *spying* on someone! Maybe I hid. What if they found me?"

He stepped forward, worry etched across his forehead. "Take a breath. You'll be okay."

"Or—no. None of this makes sense." She held her hand up as a shield to keep him away.

Unease danced in his eyes, and his chiseled jaw stiffened. "Allie—"

"Tell me!"

He stayed silent.

"Please, James," she whispered. "Tell me. Anything. You know more than you're saying. Right? Did someone hit me? Why do I feel like everything about my life is a charade? Who are you protecting?" Tears fell down her face. "Oh my God. I do sound insane."

His jaw flexed, and his dull eyes went angry. "I should go. Is that what you want?"

"No. Yes. I don't know." Allie took a step back and put her shaking hands on the dresser as she watched James dress methodically.

He turned toward her, and his eyes failed to speak the truth. "Last night was amazing, angel. One of those things we'll always have to remember." He walked over and kissed her on the cheek. "Take care of yourself. Please."

Then he left her clinging to the dresser, and her tears cascaded. Missing him already was impossible. Hurting over simple sex seemed trivial. But she couldn't stop the waterworks.

Allie dropped to her knees, wrapping herself into a ball, and let her only memory push her into a fit of desperately sad tears. Over a man she didn't know but swore she could feel in her bones. And now he was gone.

CHAPTER NINE

HOURS HAD PASSED. ALLIE'S HEADACHE had come and gone, much like James. He had been gone long enough for her tears to stop. But still she was lying there.

She pushed up and leaned against the dresser. His reaction had all but confirmed that she was right, and he was in on whatever was happening. An investigation was needed. But for who or what... she had no idea. Still, it had to start now, or she would stay on this floor forever and maybe give up hope that her past would ever come back.

"Who am I?" She had no plan, had no idea... Allie stood and walked to her utility closet. Her actions were second nature, and once she started moving, she let her feet do the thinking because she still had no clue what to do.

Her hands reached for a toolbox, and she stared at the generic plastic box. "What am I doing?"

But it was as though her subconscious had a course of action all its own. She extracted a screwdriver, a flathead, and an adjustable Allen wrench then walked to the front of her house. "What can I learn from this house?" And why did she feel as if the house should tell her anything, anyway?

Allie pressed her back up against the front door, where she'd met James hours before—and ignored the pang that tore at her heart. Then she stared at what was supposed to be her humble abode.

Her eyes swept back and forth, searching for who knew what, but her instincts screamed. Her chin dropped to her chest, and she was lost. "I'm losing my mind."

She let her gaze crawl up the wall and back down. Her sight froze on an air vent. *Bingo.* Maybe she was nuts, but it didn't matter. That was her answer. She dropped to her knees and crawled toward it. Her fingers brushed over the hardware. As quickly as she could, Allie unscrewed the vent cover and peered inside. There was nothing there. She ran her finger along the cover—only dust. She repeated the same process for every vent, outlet, and light switch cover then ran toward the kitchen, tearing it apart. The fridge was clean, the cabinets held no secret messages, and her dishwasher revealed nothing.

It took hours, and she had a fake Internet job to get to, but that didn't matter, and her instincts were real.

Four and a half hours later, every vent cover, outlet, and switch cover had been removed and inspected, but Allie had nothing. Her house was in a state of disarray. Her mind was a notch closer to hysteria. Yet she was more determined than ever to figure out what was going on.

She went back to her bedroom and grabbed her phone. There were messages from her so-called marketing friends, these people she supposedly had been working with. *Whatever.* She was just a face in a profile, somebody that had been plugged in, a warm body that had been pimped into a username. There were a few messages from Beth. She scrolled through, skimming what Beth had said. Mostly, it looked as though she wanted to get together for dinner or cocktails. Beth seemed so concerned about her transition from remembering nothing to remembering her *old life*.

And there was one text message from James.

JAMES: MAYBE ONE DAY THIS WILL MAKE SENSE FOR BOTH OF US.

Screw it. Allie grabbed her phone and shoved it into a drawer. She couldn't deal with her shredded heart and mopped away a stray tear. "I can't handle a past life and him."

Maybe one day, everything would make sense. But until then, she was going to binge on cereal and daytime TV. She poured herself a bowl of Lucky Charms and plopped onto the couch. With the remote in hand, she numbly surfed the channels and hoped some leprechaun luck would rub off.

"*The woman holds the baby,*" the man on public-access TV said.

But that wasn't English. Allie's channel-flipping thumb froze, and with her mouth full of cereal, she couldn't tear her eyes away from the man on the screen.

While the words that came out of his mouth should have been gibberish, she understood what he said. The line at the bottom of the screen simply read Yoruba—101 Public Access College Class.

The spoon fell out of Allie's mouth. It clattered on the hardwood floor as she choked on a marshmallow. "What the hell?"

The teacher spoke clearly in basic sentences that would have been in an elementary school reading primer but in a language that she should not have understood. It was a language that *most* people never came in contact with. Most colleges wouldn't even offer the language on campus, which was why it was likely being offered in this format. It was rare, yet she understood every word coming out of his mouth.

She understood so well, she could tell he was conjugating verbs.

The woman was holding the baby.

The woman will hold the baby.

The woman held the baby.

Trembling, Allie looked around the room at the vent covers she had removed and the outlets that were still exposed. Then her gaze shot back to the TV, where she understood this foreign tongue. Last night, when James had rung the doorbell, her hands had immediately gone to her waist as though she was searching for—*a weapon?*

Who was she?

What was she?

She was something, that much she knew. James knew it too.

Everything about this house was fabricated. "I have to get out of here."

Allie dropped the bowl and ran to her bedroom, going straight for the drawer and pulling out her phone. There was a new text message from James.

JAMES: THIS ENDED ALL WRONG. CAN I COME BACK AND SEE YOU?

Hell no. She dropped the phone as though he could see what had happened in the house since he had been gone. He couldn't be trusted. He was one of them, whoever *them* was. And now, finally, she was on the right track.

Allie left the phone on the floor and grabbed her running shoes, lacing them up then putting them to use. She sprinted toward her back door, stopping briefly at her purse to grab a handful of cash and her debit card. There was a convenience store a half block away. She would run there, withdraw everything she could, ditch the card, and find somewhere to exchange the cash, because if someone tracked down the bills she received from her initial withdrawal by their serial numbers, they could find where she spent them and triangulate her location.

How on earth did she know to change out the dollar bills?

Yes, she needed to know who she was.

The back door had barely slammed shut as she hit the steps and ran as fast as her legs would carry her.

CHAPTER TEN

SWEAT POURED DOWN JAMES'S UNDER Armour shirt. His arms pumped, and his lungs pounded to keep up with the grueling pace he forced himself to take. Powering harder up the trail didn't clear his mind, so he pushed but couldn't climb the Blue Ridge Mountains fast enough to escape the memory of Allie in his arms. He could never see her again. Hell... there was no forgetting her.

He growled as he reached the zenith of the mountain trail and bent over, spent. He gasped and hoped for some semblance of clarity. But there was none. He'd wanted to outrun his thoughts—but failed. He couldn't remember a time when he'd last floundered.

Sweat burned his eyes. He tasted it on his tongue. James stretched and gave up on clearing his head, pivoting to jog down the hill. The path wound down, as did his breath, but not his mind. The final turn lay ahead, and his goal to forget the girl had been in vain. Muscles loose and mind numb, James rounded the corner and came face to face with Beth. *Damn it.*

She looked as pissed as he felt about seeing her. "Hello to you too."

"Where is she?" Beth snapped.

Everything in his peripheral lurched as he tried to focus on Beth. He'd caught his breath, but his blood pressure jumped. "Allie?"

"Who else do you think I would drive two hours to ask about in person?"

"What do you mean?" If she was missing... His stomach churned, and his lactic-acid-bleary muscles were robbed of oxygen all over again.

"She cleaned out her ATM, and by the time I got to her house, *she was gone.* Every duct cover and light switch had been removed and left methodically lined up throughout her house."

"Shit." James rubbed his hands over his face and into his hair, shaking his head. "I'm not one to tell you guys how to do your business, but you're doing this wrong."

"How much does she remember?"

"Beth…" James trailed off. "When I see somebody who could easily recover memories having to force them down?" He glared. "I know it's not my business why the Agency is doing it this way, but you cannot force somebody to forget what is resurfacing."

"It's not my call." Beth crossed her arms, and her eyes narrowed. "It's a matter of national security—"

"This again? National security? If that's your goddamn issue, then you have a problem. Because she has memories resurfacing. They're coming in fast. They're coming in spurts. And now she's *missing*." He threw up air quotes, not sure if he believed anyone at this point but Allie. Regret was going to eat him alive if she was hurt and he could have prevented it.

"If they wanted her dead, they would've killed her."

If he thought his blood pressure had climbed before dealing with the CIA, now the reading would have been skyscraper-high. "You're the middleman here; I get that. But you need to talk to them—"

"Yeah, let me get right on that. *I don't talk to them,*" she spat back. "It's not a conversation. This isn't a 'kumbaya, let's figure it out.' These are orders."

"Why?"

Beth tossed her arms in exasperation. "Do you really think I've asked that question?"

James dropped his head back to look at the sky. He drank in a deep breath then leveled a stare at Beth. "I don't think you've asked it out loud, but I think you've asked it to yourself. Whether or not you two knew each other, I don't care. I don't care if you were ever friends to begin with. You know this is fucked up. You're smart enough to know a bad situation when there is one. So if you're not going to ask the powers that be? Fine. But don't expect me to help you if she's on the run."

Beth slammed the silverware drawer and stomped around her kitchen. Using the toe of her high heel, she kicked the dishwasher shut then launched a dishrag into the sink as her husband cleared his throat.

"Is there something you need to get off your chest?" Roman leaned back in his chair at the kitchen table. "Because you're gonna wake the baby. And I am not getting blamed for that shit."

Beth spun on her heel. "*What?*"

"Whoa, pretty girl!" Roman threw his hands up. "I'm innocent. Why ever you're mad, I didn't do it."

She ground her molars and pinched the bridge of her nose, massaging away tension. "I know you didn't do it."

"Then there's something wrong."

"Gee, you think?" She blew out a deep breath, failing to leave the stress of work far away from home. She rubbed her face, and guilt bubbled for snapping at Roman. Neither one of them wanted to wake the baby. "I just don't get what is going on."

"Can you talk about it?" he asked.

"Not really. Though we have the sanctity of those marriage vows and the umbrella of Titan to blame if I couldn't keep my mouth shut."

"You kicked the dishwasher over something at Titan?"

"*Not* Titan. Though Jared knows what's up." Beth bit her lip. She was out of ideas, and right or wrong, she needed Roman's advice. "My decommissioned asset is gone."

"I assume you have Farm boys hunting her down."

"You assume correctly. I think she's getting her memory back." She chewed her manicured nail.

Roman rubbed his chin. "Not surprising, right? It's not like this was a planned injury." He lifted his eyebrows questioningly.

She shook her head, agreeing with his sentiment. "No. Accident. And the woman's career is gone just like that. Please promise me that if something like that ever happens, you won't do this to me. Because I can see it in her eyes. She's going nuts trying to figure out who she was. Instinctively, she knows, but everything surrounding her tells her something different."

"Sucks."

"I'm surprised it took her days to run."

Roman nodded his agreement. "I wouldn't do you like that, babe. No worries. What she saw worth that much of a headache?"

Beth couldn't wrap her head around that question. What didn't they want her to re-learn but wouldn't eliminate her over? It wasn't Beth's place to guess, learn, or figure out. Much safer that way too. If Allie was dirty, she would be dead.

"I'll tell you this, though. I've never seen a more determined section chief."

"They want to know what she knows and who she's told. Not just now, but before she lost her memory," Roman said. "That's your answer, babe."

That was the only truth left, wasn't it?

The convenience-store cameras seemed to follow Allie, even though she knew that wasn't possible. Paranoia was eating her alive. She had to get to a different location—someplace unexpected or off the grid. It had taken her half a day to crisscross through town in a manner that she thought couldn't be tracked, which legitimately made her feel nutty. But finally, she had arrived in a store that sold prepaid cell phones, and she grabbed one off the shelf. At the counter, the clerk didn't even look at her, and it was the littlest of reassurances.

"Will that be all?" he asked.

"A prepaid debit card too, please." Allie paid in cash and opened the package before the cashier had returned her change.

She pocketed the coins and made her way out the door, trying to find somebody's free Wi-Fi to tap into. It wasn't an easy task. "Come on."

A signal popped in front of a restaurant, and she tapped in. A moment later, Allie had the Uber app downloaded and requested a free trial ride, using a fake name and untraceable profile.

Allie couldn't explain exactly where she was going or why she was drawn there, just that she had to get there. Ten minutes later, a red Jeep rolled up, and a man with a big beard rolled down the window. "Hey, am I looking for you?"

"You are." She rubbed her hands together, mumbling, "I have no idea what I'm looking for, but we'll find it together." She joined him in the Jeep. "Thanks."

"Okay, so here we go—"

"Can I give you someplace different? Same area, I promise." *I think.*

"Well…"

"It's important. I'm just looking for someplace that meant something very special to me, but I don't know the address; I just know where it is."

"Look, lady. This is a business, not a free shuttle."

"Does your business take fifties?" She reached into her pocket and shuffled through her cash. "Because that is what this is worth to me right now. I think it's a close drive."

The bearded man chuckled. "This free shuttle just became your chariot."

"Thank you." Allie slumped in her seat, taking a breath for the first moment since she had run out the door in search of an ATM. She fired off a few vague directions, and the Jeep took off. She had no idea what she would find at the end of this ride, only that it was the start, and maybe end, of everything. Minutes passed, and maybe relying on instinct and memories wasn't a great idea— "Stop! Stop, this is it."

Allie pushed up against the Jeep window, having no idea where she was. Yet she was certain she should be there. She handed over the fifty-dollar bill to the man and opened her door.

"Do you want me to wait?" he asked.

She turned back to him then searched up and down the nice street with the quiet houses and the manicured lawns. The area was well to do, with landscaped mulch beds and the occasional Volvo and Range Rover in the driveway. They were in solid suburbia. This house was so familiar that she felt as though she could walk in. She wouldn't, but she knew she had before.

"Please. I don't know how long I'll be, but I'll pay you to wait close by."

"Can do—are you expecting somebody?"

A Range Rover pulled into the driveway, and Allie's heart drummed faster. Because of the angle and the sun's glare, she couldn't tell who was in the driver's seat, but the anticipation of what was about to happen had her on pins and needles.

The garage didn't open, but the driver's door did. A slightly older but fit man exited and stared at her with a familiar ease. He leaned back against the expensive SUV, crossing his arms as if waiting for an appointment to show. She had not expected his body language to be so relaxed. It was as though he'd known she was already there.

"Hello." She silenced the "sir" she almost used to address him.

"Do you know who I am, Allie?" His eyes were assessing, as though he were running an AB analysis—what he knew of her previously and what he saw of her now. What were his results?

"I know that you have all of the answers I need." She took a step forward, trusting him and needing his counsel. Whoever he was to her, this was a safe place. A haven. "You've never led me astray before, and I need to trust that you won't now."

His trustworthy gaze broke away, and with just a nod and a glance, the man ordered her into the house. She obeyed and led the way up the sidewalk. This was business, and that was good. Because everything she'd been told to this point about her business had been a lie, and finally, she had found a lead on her own.

CHAPTER ELEVEN

EVERYTHING INSIDE THIS HOUSE SEEMED distantly familiar—the scent, the layout—even how accustomed she was to entering with him. He turned off the alarm and let her in, then tossed his keys into a little jar on a table by the door. It was as though they had a system. She stepped to the side, he would unlock, disarm, and open the door, she would step in, and here they were.

For the first time since she had been home, everything felt normal. Safe. "Did we used to date?"

He drew in a slow breath and let it out. "You still don't remember."

"And you know I have no memory, yet this is the first time I'm seeing you. Why is that?"

He didn't answer, instead walking past her toward what she knew was the kitchen. His name was on the tip of her tongue, yet she couldn't call to him. Allie followed and tried to figure out who he was to her. He was attractive. But was she attracted to him? No. She was attracted to James. Her skin lit on fire even now, as she thought about their night together. Yet her heart sank just as much as she remembered how they'd parted. If she never saw him again, it might kill her. Truthfully, what did she know? Lots of things could kill her.

Did James know this man too? Everybody knew what was going on but her. She slammed a hand against the wall. "Damn it! Why won't anybody tell me anything?"

He pivoted with one eyebrow raised. "I'm glad to see you haven't lost your fiery temper."

But that... that tone of voice. That wasn't a safe, confidence-inspiring tone. She dropped her hand to her side, opting to keep her attitude in check. "You obviously know I don't remember who you are. Could you please tell me?"

"My name is Daniel Yardman. I own several restaurants in the area, and you've done a great deal of marketing work for me. For which I am grateful. Thank you for all of your help, and I look forward to everything we'll do in the—"

"Bullshit." Another round of lies. Closer to the truth, but this was still more made-up fabrication, and she was done! The safe zone was gone, and she spun, making her way toward the door. "Never mind."

"Allie," he called to her back. "Allie."

"What!" She jerked around. "What do you want? Because I don't believe you. Because you know me, and I know you, and we both know that you aren't telling the truth. That this is some elaborate hoax—"

"If you're not feeling well, I can get help—"

"Don't you dare," she snapped.

"You need to stop." He dropped his voice low. "Let it go. Move on. You have a great life now."

Allie rushed forward. Her hand connected with his throat, and her knee jammed toward his groin. He blocked the shot, defending himself. His other hand grabbed her wrist before she could reach a pressure point, and her other arm came for his ear.

She didn't know how it was happening, but they went hand to hand. Daniel swung; she ducked. Instinct made her fly at him; training made her ferocious. He defended himself with expert finesse. She was the aggressor, handling herself against his height, his weight, and his expertise as though she were born to do this.

He bore down, and she went low. "Stop it, goddamn it, Allie."

She drew her head back and slammed it forward, smashing her forehead into his face. Instantaneously, stars spun in her head when she made contact with his teeth, and he grunted. That had to have drawn blood.

Screw with me again! Lie to me again! "Tell me!"

She shot her knee up to connect with his groin. He grabbed her forearms and slammed her against the wall. She used his hold as a fulcrum point and tucked her knees to her chest then shot out, trying to push him away.

She had no idea who she was, but hell, she could fight.

His fist flew. The asshole didn't hold back, and neither would she. Her right hook jammed under his chin. Daniel dropped forward, and she braced for the head butt, but his lips hit hers, and she froze.

Both of his hands took her cheeks, and he held her face. It was a panting, adrenaline-filled kiss. *An angry one.* And when he drew back, her fight was gone.

"Now, behave!" Daniel paced in front of her as she watched, completely dumbstruck. That was so far past unexpected that she had no reaction. It did not trigger any memories and didn't turn her on. She had no idea what it did to him, whether he was as angry as his face showed, whether they had a past they couldn't get over, or whether she couldn't remember a future they had flirted about.

Allie wiped her lips with the back of her hand, her body roiling with disgust.

Daniel stopped pacing. "Allie, we—"

She put the kiss-wiping hand up as a buffer from whatever he was about to say. Something about his tone rang loudly in her ears, and she just wanted to leave. That had nothing to do with the fight or the kiss. Maybe this was never a sanctuary. "I'm gonna head out now."

"You don't remember anything?" he asked. "No questions, concerns, ideas... nothing?"

"No," she lied, awkwardly walking to the front door. His eyes bored into her back as she let herself out. The house of answers left her only more confused than when she had come in.

CHAPTER TWELVE

"DON'T RUN. DON'T RUN." THE world was closing in on her as Allie pretended to maintain her composure while walking out of Daniel Yardman's door and situating herself into the backseat of the Jeep. Her chest was tight, and her electrified mind didn't know which way to go, though it began to spin theories. None of the top contenders were excellent options. What the hell had just happened in there?

The Uber driver pulled away from the sidewalk, stroking his out-of-control beard as the Jeep groaned under the gas pedal. "Where to now?"

She had no idea. "Do I look like an undercover cop?"

"Nope. Where are we going?" he asked, pausing at a stop sign.

"Hmm." She had just fought and kissed a man. The fighting thing was impressive, but now her muscles ached. A few bruises were sure to form, though wow... she was badass. "How about we drive around and check out some neighborhoods?"

"As long as your money spends, we can go wherever you want. Whoever did you wrong, man, I'm sorry about that. He shouldn't have. You seem like a pretty girl. Dude was a dick."

She rubbed a bruise forming on her neck. "I'm not the woman scorned."

He chuckled. "We're not looking for the other woman?"

"No." Allie buckled in. "I have amnesia. I'm trying to figure out my life."

"Well, fuck me. I feel kinda bad for taking all your money, then." He turned again. "You point, and I'll drive. We'll figure it out."

She closed her eyes. Daniel Yardman's house had been familiar, and she'd found it on instinct. She could feel her way to the next place.

For the next forty-five minutes, Allie let her instinct guide them, crosshatching down a highway, into neighborhoods that made no sense to her. "Wait!"

The Jeep slowed in front of a small, nonchalant, single-family home. It was older and, at first glance, needed a face lift. Everything about it was bland. Except she could not look away. This was home. And there was a For Sale sign in the front yard.

"Give me a minute." She unbuckled and pushed out of the Jeep. Numbly, she shut the car door and walked up the sidewalk. Her mind rushed. She couldn't catch one memory, feeling as if her mind were trying to fast-forward through a movie and everything was a blur. But a sense of familiarity descended upon her with the weight of a heavy wool blanket wrapping itself around her. It was both comforting and strangling.

Because she wasn't crazy.

Because everything that she had been told was now confirmed a lie.

All of her guesses, all of her assumptions... she'd been right.

But why? Who was she? The thoughts of what she could be ran through her head. If not an undercover cop, then what? *A spy?* All of the lies. The fake house. The fake job history. The fake friends. Her fake injuries. Her real injuries—the bumps and bruises, scrapes and scratches that she couldn't explain—that didn't match up with what she had been told had happened to her.

Maybe she'd watched too many action flicks, *not romantic comedies*, before she lost her memory. Maybe she'd read too many spy novels. Maybe she was a conspiracy theorist? But conspiracy theorists worked alone. And who was Beth? Who was James? Why were there so many people actively lying to her?

These were not little problems. And the house standing before her versus the house that she'd been told was hers... that was not a small inconsistency. That was a major, financial issue that somebody was paying for. As she stood on the front step of what she knew was her house, Allie ran her hand alongside the front door then looked under the mat for a key. There was a realtor's lockbox hanging from the doorknob, but she found no spare key for entry. With a quick glance over her shoulder, Allie saw the Uber driver watching her intently. *Shit.* If she was anywhere near right about what was going on, she had dragged him into something he did not need to be a part of.

She gave him a quick wave, and he waved back. Then she walked along the familiar side of the house to a back door. Well, hell, she was there now, and she wouldn't be there for long. What did she have to lose? She pressed her back against the back door and pushed her elbow against the old glass pane. With a quick glance around, she knew that nobody could see her and drew back her elbow, broke the glass pane, then quickly popped her hand in and unlocked the door from the inside. "It's my place, anyways…"

She opened the door slowly, relieved that no alarm went off. Not that she could hear. *Shit.* What if she *was* a spy?

Worse, what if she wasn't? She had just broken into a house and was certifiable! Her heart slammed in her chest.

Walking in, Allie took a breath to slow her heart rate, and the same familiarity struck her again. Memories rushed at her, and finally, a clear one hit. She closed her eyes, squeezing them tight. One vivid picture of an old 1970s kitchen with avocado appliances stuck out in her mind. The floor was linoleum and slightly yellow tinged. Everything was very clean but straight out of the '70s. Her hands started to shake as she followed the path that she knew would take her to the kitchen. Allie rounded the corner, and there it was. Staring back at her was the green refrigerator. Everything in this room matched what had just been in her mind.

This was her kitchen.

And if she was a spy, this was a CIA cleanup job—a *CIA cleanup job?* Cleanup job… What did that mean? *Think.* A team would have come in to erase her old life. Would they monitor if somebody still came into the old house? She didn't know or couldn't remember. Either way, she didn't have much time. Allie tore through the house, not sure what she was looking for. But some things looked familiar, and other things were blank. Either way, this was her past-life confirmation—and it was making her heart race.

"Calm down! Think clearly!"

Allie went to the farthest part of the house, what had to be a guest bedroom, and methodically worked her way through each room. She noticed things that perhaps a normal person wouldn't have noticed. For such an old house, all of the light switch covers had recently had the screws turned, as evidenced by the broken paint and occasional new screws. She wouldn't waste time looking where other people had already been. If she had been smart and wanted to hide something, it would have been with the purpose of avoiding a professional cleanup team.

Allie worked through the house, running her hands everywhere, checking the top of the crown molding, and pulling up the edges of the carpet that seemed a tiny bit loose. There was nothing, no clues and no answers.

Finally, she ended up in the kitchen again. The answer had to be in this room. The linoleum floor hadn't been pulled up and reapplied. She had checked on top of the cabinets, inside them, and as much as she could under them. There was nothing to see except for the ugly appliances that she almost liked. Maybe if she had been a spy on the run, doing who knew what, traveling who knew where, she would have found them comforting, as she did now.

If she *was* going to leave a clue or an answer for herself—not that she would have known she would get amnesia—but if she was going to hide information, back up her data, or store intel, she would have done it with these ugly-ass appliances.

There wasn't a dishwasher, just an oven, a separate electric range top, and a refrigerator.

She opened the fridge and ran her hands along the doors. She checked the drawers and pulled them out. Nothing. Funny—she found the kitchen most comforting, considering she couldn't cook. There had once been a microwave in there, and it had served to cook every meal. Wait—the stove and the oven were never used. Goose bumps erupted over her skin, and she knew she was about to figure out everything.

She pulled the coils out of the stovetop and then went to the oven beside the stove and pulled the heating elements out. Some elements were faceup, others facedown. But the answers were right there. "Holy crap."

She didn't know what it meant, but that was her handwriting. Written in what appeared to be fine-point chalk that she had just smudged slightly were random words. They didn't form sentences and didn't make sense. But they were in her handwriting, and they were her answer.

CHAPTER THIRTEEN

WITH THE HEATING ELEMENTS FROM a 1970s house gathered under her arm, Allie ran out the back door, trying carefully not to smudge any of the chalk. But she was aware now that she had a semi-photographic memory, because she could not unsee those words. The Jeep driver's eyes were wide. It occurred to her that she should get his name, because they were about to enter a different level of their newfound relationship. Most notably, he was perhaps an accomplice.

Balancing everything in an arm, she opened the door. "Hey, time to go." And as best she could, she put all the metal cooking elements by her side without letting them tangle. "Don't mind me; I will explain. By the way, my name is Allie. And yours?"

"Not sure I signed up to be Bonnie and Clyde. I thought this was about finding your past."

"This is my past," she said as way of a nonexplanation.

"You stole somebody's stove!"

Allie had no idea why she did this but it was important to her once. "There's an oven element here too. Not just the stovetop."

"Oh, well. If it's the oven, too, I guess that makes a difference." He shifted out of park.

A white van screeched around the corner, and Allie's eyes went straight to it. "You should go. Now. Now!"

"Who is *that*?"

"I don't know." But unsteady nerves gurgled in her stomach. That wasn't just any old bad driver. It was someone on a mission to find out why she had just been in that house. "Just go!"

"Jesus." He shifted the Jeep into drive and slammed down the gas pedal. The SUV wasn't made to be a speed rocket getaway vehicle, and the engine roared in angry protest before it hopped to and tried its best to catch up.

She was far in over her head and needed to let her driver off the hook. As much as she didn't want to trust anyone, there was one person she should try to trust again.

"I need to call James. He'll know what to do." She reached for the burner phone—and realized she had no idea how to get ahold of him. "Shit."

The Jeep screeched around the corner. "Who are those people? Hell. Who are you, lady?"

"I don't know. I've been trying to figure it out. And those people don't want me to remember. But James knows."

"Well, call James already," he shouted at her as he took the next turn like a pro.

"I don't have his phone number. I don't even know where he lives. All I know is that he's a doctor at Summerland Hospital."

"I've got this. Hey, Siri—Wait, what's the guy's name?"

Siri turned on and explained that she did not know who the driver was talking about.

"His name is James Tuska," Allie explained. "And he's a physician at the hospital."

"Hey, Siri, call Summerland Hospital." A moment later, the phone's dial tone then ringing sounded through the Jeep's speakers. The hospital switchboard answered.

The driver, whom she still didn't have a name for, did all the talking, and she was impressed by how cool under pressure the guy was and by how well he drove. While he demanded to speak to Dr. Tuska about a vague, nonexistent medical emergency, she turned over all the heating elements and tried to make sense of the words. Nothing jogged a memory; it was hopeless.

"I'm sorry, sir. He is not available," the operator continued to explain.

After another back and forth, the driver left his phone number and demanded an emergency callback from Dr. Tuska, then he turned to her in the mirror. "Do you think he'll call?"

Allie bit her lip. "I have no idea."

They rounded another corner, the tires squealing in protest, as the phone rang. It buzzed in its holder, which was connected to an air vent on the front of the dashboard, so she could read the display. The call came up as an unknown number.

Allie held her breath as the driver answered. "Hello?"

"This is Dr. James Tuska returning an emergency phone call. Can I help you?"

The Jeep driver looked over his shoulder, and she had one shot to either make James believe her or at least make him fess up as much of the truth as she could get him to give her. "I've started remembering; I've found things. I went to my old house. And now they're after me!"

"Allie?"

"And her Uber driver," said the man behind the wheel, "who is still at this point remaining nameless. And I can vouch for her. There are people chasing us." He screeched around another corner.

"Allie, where are you?"

Her instincts told her not to say that out loud, and she shook her head. "I can't say that over the phone."

"I wouldn't either," said the Jeep driver. "I know this area like the back of my hand, and I'm spinning them in a thousand different ways. If they can't see me, they won't find us. But I wouldn't say out loud where we are. This lady's smart. Even if she can't remember shit."

"Allie," James said with all the seriousness that she had hoped he would give this phone call. He believed her. He was going to do something or tell her something. "It is best for your safety if you stop all of this silliness."

Her heart tumbled as he let her down. "Please don't say that. I don't know what you know, but whatever it is can save my life, not just my memory."

They came to a stop sign, and the driver turned and looked at her. "What do you want to do?"

She wanted to run and hide. She wanted to cry. More than that, she wanted to get angry and shout at James for not helping. But he was just a one-night stand with whom she happened to have incredible chemistry. He was her sexy doctor whom she'd pretended to love once upon a time but could see how loving him now would be entirely possible... because maybe they had more than just chemistry, and... maybe she had dreamed about more than a one night stand. "If he's not with us, he's against us. Hang up."

"Us?" The Jeep driver balked. "I'm not on your team. I'm your Uber driver."

Still, they sat at a stop sign in the middle of suburbia with no traffic coming either way. "You're more than that. I don't know your name, but you're more helpful than the guy on the phone." A thousand tiny stings bit into her throat at the size of that lie.

"Not so sure after you broke into a house and stole shit."

"You did what?" James broke in, nearly shouting.

"It was her house, buddy. Like the lady said, you're either with us or against us. If you're against us, you don't get to ask questions. If you're with us, you can ask questions. 'Cause I don't know what to ask her."

"I found my old house, James. And I found—I can't say it on the phone—but I found it. And I will figure out whatever *it* is."

James blew into his phone, and his frustration echoed in the Jeep. "Allie, do you know that place that was in that movie we watched? Where I said I spent time working when I needed to get away from the noise of the hospital? It's near your house—the house I visited. Not the other one you—"

"That she broke into," the driver said, and she smirked.

James ignored him. "Meet me there, and we'll talk face to face."

Why did James want to go there? It didn't matter; she needed to see him.

"Do you want to meet him?" the driver asked. "Or do you even know what he's talking about?"

She did, and her pulse pounded in her throat. "Thank you, James."

The Jeep driver disconnected the call. "Where are we headed?"

"Summerland U's medical campus."

"The university's med school? You got that from what he just said?"

"Yup."

"This is straight out of a book. No one will ever believe me." He flicked on his turn signal and eased on the gas, making a left turn.

Allie had no idea what they would do there, but in the meantime, she went back to the tiny words written in chalk and tried to figure out the word puzzle she had left herself in case of emergency.

CHAPTER FOURTEEN

THE JEEP SCREECHED AWAY AFTER a quick wish of good luck from the driver. Allie found herself walking from the parking lot onto the semi-busy medical campus of Summerland University. A map greeted her and easily pointed her to the academic and professional buildings that James had mentioned. After just a few turns on campus, there he was, waiting for her and leaning against the brick entryway.

With the danger swirling around her, it was the wrong time to take a moment and appreciate how ruggedly handsome James was. Posted against the wall of the imposing medical facility with his arms crossed, he was either glaring at her or simply studying her walk up the sidewalk—she couldn't tell which. But there was seriousness about his demeanor, protectiveness about his stance. Whether or not he was angry with her? She had no idea. Why would he be? Except for the fact that she had broken into a house and defied his "doctor's order" to take care.

"You showed," Allie mumbled, unsure of where she stood with him.

"You gave me little choice. What was I supposed to do? You said people were chasing you."

What was she carrying? And why was he here? Simple… he couldn't stay away. And that had nothing to do with how smart and beautiful she was. That had to do with a sense of responsibility that he had to her safety and to her health.

Her gaze shifted uneasily. "Who did I work for? Can you please tell me what I already know?"

"Allie, that is not why I'm here."

"Then why are you here?" Her exhausted voice hit him with fear and frustration.

"I had to make sure you were safe." Beth had called and said Allie had attacked a section chief before going to her old house. That wasn't the woman James knew, and he wanted to hear Allie's side of the story.

"I won't be safe until I stop them. And you know who they are. It's the CIA, isn't it?"

His shoulders twitched. There was so much to say yet so much he did not know. "That's a hell of a leap, Allie—"

"Dammit, James!"

He dropped his voice low. "Angel."

"Do not be sweet to me."

What the hell was he going to do? They were just standing here on campus, and he could feel looks from the passersby at the odd things she held.

"Why are you holding kitchen… stuff?" Because if this was why she'd broken into a house that she claimed was hers? Maybe they had bigger issues to deal with. If she was stealing people's stovetops, maybe she needed to be seen by her brain trauma specialist again.

"Don't look at me like that. Like I'm nuts." Allie started to back up and guarded the pieces of the stolen kitchen appliances as though they were a life preserver saving her from a crazy nightmare. "I already said you're either with me or against me."

"Can you explain what you're holding to me, then?"

She shrugged defensively.

"Let's go inside. I'm not here to judge you. Just… help."

Relenting, Allie let him lead the way as they ducked inside the building. He casually waved at a resident that he couldn't ignore and kept walking. They needed to get to his secure office, where they could speak in private.

"Whoa, Doc." A security guard he'd seen off and on for the past several years waved him down. "ID? Where's the badge?"

Shit. "I didn't expect to be here today."

The guard shook his head. "You know the rules. No ID, no entrance. Can't let you past this door."

Allie wheeled around. "Let's go."

"Hang on," James said. They needed privacy immediately, and the CIA would know where she was by now, but not necessarily in which building or room. She didn't need to go traipsing all over campus. They needed to get into his private office *now* before she caused a scene. As soon as they got beyond the guard, they would be off the grid. A green zone of sorts.

And… really, he needed time with his woman. Being by her side was killing him. Was it too red-blooded asshole male that he wanted to grab her to his chest and just feel her—sans the metal coils in her hand? "I need fifteen minutes to grab paperwork for a presentation I'd forgotten—"

"But…" The guard tilted his head toward her. "I can't let students up in the offices."

Allie painted on a megawatt smile. "I'm not. I'm his fiancée."

Damn it. That wasn't going to help matters.

"*Really?*" The guard's impassive face softened. "Congrats, Doc. I had no idea."

"It's new," James managed to say, unnerved and enthusiastic about a nonexistent engagement. Since when did so many people care about his social life? Allie tucked herself under his arm, oven pieces and all. "She is. We're the happy couple. *Though late.* And I have to get upstairs."

The guard stepped to the side. "Nice to meet you…"

"Corinne." Allie beamed and bounced up to give James a lingering kiss.

"Nice to meet you, Corinne," the guard said, repeating her fake name as though it were the best news he'd heard all day. "ID next time, Doc, and congrats."

Whatever the guard said didn't matter. Allie's chaste kiss was like smoldering fire on James's skin. The innocent peck could have been her stripping naked for the reaction his body had to the caress. Stiffly, he cleared his throat. "Thanks. Will do."

They moved down the guarded hallway, and she brushed against him. "Fiancée was quick on my tongue. Sorry if I shouldn't have said that. Though I kind of like the name Corinne. That fell off my tongue too."

"You're fine." Hell, this woman. He'd known her for a couple of weeks, slept with her only once, but Allie was an addiction. The kiss and the title of "fiancé" did absurd things to him, lighting a craving he could barely control. He liked it. Liked her. Wanted her. Why did they have to meet like this?

"Then why did you startle when I said we were engaged?"

Startle? He was more enamored with each passing step. "It wasn't a bad reaction, Allie."

Her cheeks pinked. "Oh."

And that response was a beautiful one. "The kiss was an unexpected bonus."

Abruptly, she turned and pressed her silky lips to his again, murmuring,

"To the happy couple."

He opened his mouth, owning the kiss. It couldn't be helped. She tasted like the sun, and he needed that since he'd been without her. They were the happy, turned-on, toeing-the-edge-of-danger couple. With the metal coils pressed between them, he didn't care who walked by. It wouldn't stop him now. James backed her against the wall and trying to keep his composure was a joke. "You have a thing about surprise kisses."

"Do I? Maybe." Her nimble tongue licked his bottom lip.

That didn't help. Nibbling back, he wished they were still at her house, that they had never gotten dressed, that he had never jumped into the shower. "I want back in your bed."

She nodded. "I want you there too."

Mmm. He kissed her sweet lips. "Want to talk about the break-in, or can I keep kissing you?"

"Kissing."

He laughed as the stove coils shifted between them. "Want a hand with those?"

"No." She twisted away suddenly as though he weren't allowed to touch. "Lead the way, Doc. Where can I put these down to keep them safe?"

Okay… he wouldn't offer to touch those again. "My office." And he wanted to get there fast if those coils kept distance between their bodies. They rounded to a stairwell door. "Couple flights instead of the elevator. Just in case?"

"You're a smart one," she said. "Then back to kisses until you fess up that I'm a spy."

Maybe a nonanswer wouldn't count against his security clearance. James neared the point of not caring. "Nonstop kisses coming your way."

❤

"What are you looking at?" Allie's cheeks felt warm with the promise of James's nonstop kisses in her mind.

As they ascended the stairs, his capable hands were on her waist. They were in a rush, and she had been in danger. But with his palms covering her sides and him at her back, she could appreciate that she was finally safe with a man who wanted to make her feel good.

"Nothing."

"I can feel your eyes on me," she teased.

"You're in front of me." But his long fingers flexed possessively into her sides, and her insides corkscrewed. "Are you thinking dirty thoughts?"

She couldn't take another second without exploding from the inside out and twirled around, letting James push into her breasts. "I can feel you looking at me. What's a girl to think?"

He grinned devilishly. "It's a nice view, angel."

Her tingling cheeks went from warm to on fire. Even when she pulled bold moves like this, when he dropped lines that made her insides curl and spin, she couldn't think. "I'm sorry about how we left things before. At my fake house."

"Fake house." His lips quirked. "You're so certain."

"That I never lived there? Yes." She nodded, eyeing his strong jaw and sexy eyes. As much as she wanted to remain focused, she also couldn't help but notice the obvious. James made her panties melt. "As certain as I was that you were staring at me more than you were paying attention to your surroundings."

"You've got a great ass."

"*James!*"

He chuckled, and her reaction didn't seem to bother him any. He looked over her shoulder, and when his gaze came back to her face, the humor was gone. In its place was toe-curling desire. Hunger rested in his eyes, easy and patient, just like the man she'd grown to know so well in such a short amount of time.

"Want to know what I was thinking?" His low voice rumbled and she trembled.

"Yes." Allie nodded, her breath feeling short in her chest.

"It wasn't about everything that's been going on. Maybe that makes me an asshole…"

Her nipples tightened. *Everything* tightened. With her mind in a thousand places other than where it should have been, given the day's circumstances so far, she embraced the rush of her blood, loving how high she felt as James leaned closer. His warm breath tickled her, and the anticipation of longing was almost stronger than she could handle. "*It? What were you thinking?*"

He inched even closer, and this time, she could feel the warm weight of his body too. His torso and erection pressed against her, and she swallowed away another vivid burst of arousal.

"You on your couch. Under me, Allie." His ravenous eyes had her transfixed as his thoughts swept her off her feet. "Your soft thighs wrapped around my hips."

She parted her quivering lips, giving a quiet, "Oh."

He licked his plump bottom lip, and she wanted to do that too. "I thought about those light eyes staring up at me, and I lost myself in the memory of what happened under that blanket."

"Not an asshole." Allie was almost in a pant; her hips slightly swaying. "How would thinking about us in bed be a bad thing?"

James dipped his head so that his mouth rested below her ear. The heat from his breath scored her like hot embers. "You're begging for information, and all I can think about is making you orgasm."

She whimpered and had a visceral daydream of his fingers inside her pussy.

"See," he teased with his lips against her earlobe. "Doesn't sound like I'm a good man. Even now. You asked me to find you. Help you. And fuck it if all I want to do is get you off against the wall so I can hear you come and have something to think about later."

Allie dropped her head back, needing her swollen clit to have his attention. Her wild heart slammed in her chest, and damn, she couldn't breathe for how deliriously turned on she was.

"Trust me." He rubbed his erection between them, and everything she held in her arms was in the way. "Put these down for a second. No one will touch them. I won't let them. I promise."

She nodded, believing James. With his help, the heating elements clattered to the next step.

James was a predatory man on a mission to touch her. Her breaths hitched as he slowly leaned in. "I meant to ask you about that date you were unsure about. How about dinner soon?" He confidently pushed his hand down the front of her pants and under the layer of silk to find her wet for him. "Damn, that's my angel."

She groaned as he stroked her skillfully. "Can't say things like that—and not—mmm…"

With devious tricks, he rubbed her needy clit, and the danger of getting caught—on several levels—spiked her arousal. "James. Anyone"—she closed her eyes as his adept fingers teased her slit—"could catch us."

"Keep listening. But don't be quiet." He speared her, sinking knuckle-deep inside her canal until she went dizzy. "You sound like heaven."

"Oh God," she gasped.

"Good, like that." In and out, his finger pumped as he stayed inches from her face, holding her eyes.

Allie's jaw hinged open, and her quiet moans might kill her from lack of oxygen. "James…"

He took her to the edge, giving no relief as she climbed toward the peak she craved. James curled his finger slightly, and still, he wouldn't look away, barely blinking. The man might not have breathed, either. She couldn't. Maybe it was fair that they both died for this climax.

The palm of his hand pressed against her clit, and he delved another finger inside her, methodically teasing her g-spot.

"God!" Allie tumbled against him and came.

They both jumped at voices from the stairwell above. James righted her and gave her a devious smile. "We should get going."

No! She didn't want to take her hands off of him, much less move. Her limp legs could barely hold her up, let alone climb another flight of stairs. But as the roll of fireworks in her blood subsided, a burst of energy tsunamied behind. "I'll get you back."

"Good." He pulled the door open when they reached the top of the landing. "I can't wait."

CHAPTER FIFTEEN

"THIS IS MY OFFICE WHEN I'm here. Which isn't much. But…"
James unlocked the door, and Allie walked to the window then did a quick three-sixty.

"Private and nice."

The hospital's office—his working office—was nice. But this one on campus came with the job of semester lectures and access to research facilities when he wanted them, and it still had a nice view of the school grounds. There wasn't much in the way of creature comforts, but there was a table. Allie beelined for it and laid out all the items from what looked like a stovetop and an oven. She turned the black metal pieces over, and on the underside of each was what looked like tiny words written in fine-point white lettering, though some words were smudged.

"What does it say?" He inched closer and took in the words. They were names or lists perhaps? He pulled out his phone and searched a few words then tried to connect them with an "and." Nothing relative in his choice of combinations came up.

She alternated between the coils and gave up.

"My training is coming back. Between finding my house and my old boyfriend? Who the hell knows what he was—"

"Excuse me?" Because if Allie "attacking a section chief" had anything to do with her confusion over an ex-boyfriend, he was going to have a problem with how the Agency was choosing to play their games and utilize their resources.

Allie spent the next two minutes recounting how she had shown up at Daniel Yardman's, their fight and kiss, and how she'd taken off after he'd oddly let her go.

"He asked if you remembered anything?" James took two fingers and put them on her chin, tilting her head back then dragging the collar of her shirt down. Anger boiled as he inspected her bruises. "That was it?"

Allie's eyelashes fluttered. "I lied, said no, and was on my way."

Who was he…

"I'm fine, James." As her head dipped back, his focus should have been on where her neck met her shoulder or on her collarbone, anywhere but her lips.

"You're sure?"

All he could hear was the soft sigh that whispered past on a breath. "Promise."

Awareness surrounded them, and he took a step forward, letting his fingers run along the line of her jaw. "I want to help you… as much as I want to kiss you again."

He closed the distance between their stomachs, and his hand curled around her head, his fingers threading into her hair.

"Is it possible to miss somebody I just met," she whispered, "as much as I missed you?"

His thumb rubbed back and forth in her hair as though motioning the answer yes.

"I need to ask you one question," she said. "And no matter what, you need to tell me the truth. Please, it's about you and me."

He lifted his chin in a silent okay.

"Did we know each other before? In whatever my previous life was? This connection, this chemistry that we have… It's very strong. And I can't explain it other than we knew each other before. Did we?"

James had done so much work for so many intelligence organizations, private security groups, and every combination of joint-operative task forces that could be thought of. This woman was unforgettable. "No, Allie. If you had been mine before, no amount of orders could keep me away from you."

Her eyes sealed shut, and he dipped his mouth to hers, brushing the most earnest kiss he could promise across her lips.

"Mm-hmm." She swayed into him.

"I can't keep my hands off of you." His certain plan to get her off so he would have something to think about later was a disaster.

"I don't want you to stop." She held onto his shoulders. "So that works well for us."

Sweet and on an adrenaline high, her blend of wild and sexy intoxicated him. "You've had a whirlwind day."

"I learned earlier I can fight a man." Allie tilted her neck and let him nuzzle. "And win."

Now, it was his turn to groan. "I don't like hearing that."

Still, he wanted to get to the bottom of the boyfriend mystery. If she had an ex from the CIA, why hadn't that been part of what Beth had told James, and why wasn't he brought in on the project?

"Those hands are losing their focus, James."

He drew back. "Remember why we're here."

"To keep me happy and safe." Her eyebrows bobbed expectantly.

"Yes. *Safe.*" He drew in a tempering breath, needing to slow his rushing blood, and tried to establish some decorum. "To talk about what you found and maybe why you're walking around with kitchen parts."

Her flushed cheeks and wild eyes were having none of his slowdown. Tension knitted between them as she barely inched back and whispered, "It has to be a doctor thing."

"What?"

Allie gave a quiet laugh, tilting her head and letting strands of hair obscure her gaze. "Your keen discipline."

"What are you talking about?"

"Who gets a woman off, teasing her to the point that she's going to lose her mind, and then wants to talk about work?"

He had no answers. "It's not work. Not mine, at least."

"When I'm with you, I forget about all of this for a little while." She rested her hands on his chest, letting her fingers gently knead his shirt. "Do you have any idea how awful it is to lose your mind and then have it come back in pieces?"

Hesitantly, he shook his head. "No."

"You save me from my mind."

"You broke into a house—"

"My house," she pointed out. Her fingers scratched his shirt. "Focus on me, Doctor. I'm asking as nicely as I can. Almost begging."

"Allie…" *Almost begging…* He knew how her addictive kisses tasted and how she would feel when he guided himself into her. They were alone, and he needed her more than she knew. "You're acting like I don't want you."

"I know you do." Allie ignored everything he said and rested her hand on his belt.

She pulled the leather loose. "You can have me."

He swallowed the knot in his throat and took over, unfastening it. "You're not bluffing, angel, are you?"

Her light eyes flared, and her lips parted. Wispy breaths poured over her lips. "No. Never."

James took her mouth, her tongue, and owned her needy moans. Her hands were pressed between them, and her short fingernails bit into his pecs. The ravaging kiss boiled his blood. He threaded his hand further into her hair, tugging to deepen the kiss, and he groaned as she backed them to the edge of a table.

"I'm going to take your sweet pussy," he promised against her lips.

"Yes, please." Allie murmured her pleading agreement. Her hips gyrated against his, and she dropped her hand to his pants, unfastening the zipper and stroking his engorged shaft through the fabric.

"Pants." She pushed them off her hips, kicking a foot free. He let his fall and lifted her onto the edge of the table.

"Cold!" Her giggles exploded until he had the head of his cock pressed to her warm, wet entrance. Everything about her changed, and the heat from her slick pussy went straight through him.

He wasn't going to make it; he was going to die. Her bare skin on his? James rubbed the crown of his hard-on over her. "Fuck, angel."

He nudged the tight area as she sucked in her breath. *Sweet Jesus.* He'd never had sex without a condom. They should talk. It was a couple thing. He shouldn't know her medical history, but hell, he did, and he wanted his dick in her so bad, he couldn't breathe.

"More," she begged.

"I don't have any protection." *Damn it. Damn it. Goddamn it.*

"I'm on birth control, and you'd tell me if we couldn't. Wouldn't you?"

"True."

Allie leaned forward and kissed him. "I knew from the moment I laid eyes on you that you'd never hurt me."

"Of course I wouldn't." A possessive need unfurled inside him. He couldn't wait another second. "Wait."

"No."

"Hold on." James's mind screamed at the faith she put in him. It had nothing to do with health and wellness but everything else. "God, Allie. Wait."

"*What?*"

"I know things about your past. I do. Goddamn it. I have a security clearance. I don't want to hurt you. In any way." He squeezed his eyes shut. "I don't think I know anything you don't already know. And nothing I know matters to you right now. I believe that."

She couldn't have been in a more vulnerable state. Why would she believe him, trust him... James was going to lose her for doing the right thing—

"I need you." She reached between them and stroked his shaft, stealing his soul. "Take me. Please. You have no idea what you do to me."

He thrust once. It was a hungry and desperate act—one that she groaned and gasped for more of. Her bare, slick skin on his... she'd stolen his thoughts and pulled her knees up, giving him a deeper angle.

Allie clung to him. "Yes."

He drew back and plunged deep again, and she wrapped her arms around him. Her knees went higher, and her incoherent gasps, he swore, sounded like *thank you*.

Seated inside the woman he never wanted to let go, James pressed his forehead to hers. "Good?"

"Just like that."

He was done for. With one swoop, he had her off the table and against the wall, making the ungraceful path with his pants around his ankles as hers fell off the foot the pant leg had dangled from. "Still good?"

"Better." Allie locked her mouth to his.

He drew back and fucked her, deep and long, sliding his length out to the tip just to drive home again. She bounced in his arms, her tits swaying under her shirt. What he wouldn't have done to have her dark pink nipple on his tongue, but the look on her face was ecstasy.

"I'm going to—" She dropped her head back and yanked it up.

He pinned her—too tight, he didn't know—until her legs locked around his back. Sweat tickled his brow. His muscles ached. Her pussy clenched his cock, and sweet Jesus, he was going to die if he couldn't feel her ripple as he spurted inside her.

"*Yes,*" Allie moaned as her body clamped around him.

He drove deep, giving her short, choppy fucks, and came so hard, he went shaky. The hot sensation of his climax coating his cock, filling her up, had more electricity to it than he could've dreamed. Like a flash of lightning, it reinvigorated her climax as well, and he swore to God, the woman started to come again. He slid in and out of her until she went lax in his arms and her lips lingered against his.

Carefully, he set her down after she untangled her legs, and he kept a steady hand on her. The la-la look on her face did all kinds of things to his ego, but his chest was what squeezed and did something even better for him. Allie gave him a thousand types of feelings that no medical book could describe.

"You good?" he asked again before righting his pants and snagging hers to hand over.

"If you didn't swear, I'd bet my life that we knew each other before."

"You keep saying that." Maybe some things were just meant to be...

CHAPTER SIXTEEN

T HERE WAS A GAME JAMES played when he was a kid. Someone would fold a piece of paper into an origami finger-game, and based on the number picked, his future would be dictated. Who he would marry, how many kids, the type of car he would drive, and where he would live. At this moment, that was how his mind felt. But there was one woman in play, and he wanted to know what the future held with Allie. The how, when, and where were the only unknowns.

"What should we do when all this is over?" he asked. "Other than dinner?"

Allie's hair partially covered her cheek. "Massages."

"Deal. Massages. And then… vacation?"

"I'm down for a vacation." Her lyrical laughter rang out—the window cracked with a whiz as the wall thumped. James pivoted side to side, seeing a spiderweb of glass and then a bullet hole in the wall.

His mind screamed gunshot as both of their training kicked in. They dove onto the ground, rolling toward the wall. No gunshot sound had rung out—there was just a shattered window and a bullet now lodged in the wall. Hell! This was a college campus. Not a place for gunfire and silencers!

Temper boiling, he tried to control his temper. "You okay?"

"Yeah. You?" She rolled up and onto the balls of her feet. She was a spy in action, surveilling the scene.

He moved to the opposite side of the room and perched in a corner. If they could get to his car without being seen, they would at least have a head start before their pursuer followed. Then he could call Beth and Titan and shut this shit show down.

She crept to the table and swept up the heating elements then placed the coils on the floor and studied them on her hands and knees.

"Allie, *get down.* What are you doing?" He ducked underneath the window and tried to grab her out of the way.

She shooed him away with one arm, concentrating on the words. Even if she thought she did great under pressure, this was pushing it a little. What more was she going to come up with right now? Not much.

"Come on," he urged. "We have to move."

"Hang on," she mumbled, dragging the words out. Then she spit-wet a thumb and wiped down the pieces, rubbing them until they were clean, dry, and free of writing. "All right. I'm good now."

Well, good. Since she was good now. Since they were being shot at. He grabbed her hand and dragged her down the hall. "Not sure that was the best time for that, but whatever."

"Semi-photographic memory. But it's triggering something. It's on the tip of my tongue. I was just trying to remember everything before we left. I can't... I want to say something, and I can't figure out what it is." Frustration held heavy in her words as she clung to his hand.

He honestly couldn't imagine the way she felt right now, compounding it all with somebody shooting at them. She had to feel more than frustration, more than irritation; it had to be straight-up, one hundred percent, pissed-off aggravation. They turned down a hall, and he saw a staircase that would take them toward the back of the building, where his car was.

As they began to make their way down the stairs, his phone buzzed. *Not the best timing.* They pressed up against the wall and silently listened. They both listened and heard nothing except his phone. Dammit, it began to buzz again. Allie gave him a look as he reached for it. It was Beth. He held the phone out so she could see it. He'd wanted to call Beth, anyway.

"What does she want?" Allie shook her head, irritated, but then she sliced a glance back at the phone as he went to answer it. "And why is she saved in your phone?"

"She's not who you think she is." He pressed the screen and answered the call then held the phone to his ear. "You need to pull your shooter off of me right now. I have Allie with me. Whatever your problem is, I do not care. Call them down. Do it *now.*"

"Excuse me?" Beth feigned surprise, which stoked his anger.

"No bullshit, Beth. I'm done with the Farm boy games. Call it off now."

A pregnant second hung in the air. "Doc, I'm telling you the truth. We have no orders to take out any assets. I have specific instructions to bring her in. That's it."

Allie cleared her throat, and he looked over. She tilted her head down the stairs. It'd been far too long since he was in the field doing any sort of operational training, and much longer since somebody with a gun was after his ass. Even when he had been there, he was staying alive to keep other people alive. As an elite soldier with medical capabilities, he had knocked on death's door. This spy–operative–rogue bullshit that was happening right now? Not his thing, nor his specialty. But he knew they needed to rock and roll, and they had no time to talk to Beth anymore. He ended the call without another word, slipped the phone into his pocket, and listened for whatever she might have heard.

Zip. He didn't hear a footstep or an echo. "What's up?"

Someone opened a door to the stairwell but didn't come up.

"Whoever it is just came inside," she whispered. "There's two of us and one of them. They want me; it's safer for you if we split up."

He almost snorted at her asinine suggestion. "Like that's going to happen." He took her capable hand and started them down the stairs, but a door opened to another level. "Maybe someone who was supposed to be here?"

"Like staff or a student."

"Makes more sense. Who knows anymore," he grumbled. His anger was subsiding to irritation as logic fault for its rightful place in the plan building process.

"James, I heard you talk about the CIA."

"Nothing you haven't already guessed. Come on, angel. Let's go." They took the two flights quietly until they finally reached the base of the stairwell. Outside the door, one way would lead back to the guard who was drastically unprepared to deal with a CIA sharpshooter, and the other, out the exit-only side of the building. That was where there were fewer people, and it was closer to his Range Rover.

"When we get out of here, where are we going to go?" she asked.

He kissed the top of her head. "I was thinking Turks and Caicos sounds like the best spot."

"I was thinking more of an immediate plan." She tried to hide an inopportune laugh. "Though I like your optimism. We're weaponless, and your car isn't sitting right outside the door, right? So... got a plan, Doc?"

"No. My car's in the closest lot. We get there. That's my plan unless you have a plan?" Because he would have taken suggestions at any point now. "You're the unconfirmed spy. I'm just the doctor."

"Yeah, I think we both know you're a little more than that. My plan is"—she bit her bottom lip and shook her head—"we run like hell, zigzag, and don't get hit."

"Let's do it, angel." With one arm, he swooped her back and swung the door open, ready to kill any attacker with his bare hands. Seeing none, they rushed and split up. And as their handhold tore apart, he wanted to shout to her to be careful, to stay safe. He wanted to tell her that he loved her, and right then, he knew that he was losing his mind just like she had lost hers.

CHAPTER SEVENTEEN

THERE WERE ONLY A FEW hundred yards between the back side of their building and where James had parked his Range Rover. The two of them looked insane running side to side, and if he hadn't known that someone with a gun was trying to kill them, or at least her, he would've thought it mattered.

But at this second, he didn't give two shits how crazy they looked as they powered off the asphalt platform, making tight Z-strides toward their rendezvous location while covering the most amount of ground in the most efficient way possible. If they had run in a straight line, they would be a shooter's dream come true. But getting the line of sight on some-body moving back and forth at different intervals at different speeds... that would be harder and maybe save their lives.

They had only a few more yards to go, and it was as if they were bot-tlenecking toward the same spot. In his mind, he knew it was the most dangerous part of their exit strategy. Intentionally, he was slowing down. "Run, Allie, harder. Harder."

She did. *Good girl. Run, angel.* He pushed her in his mind. The muffled sound of a gunshot echoed a hair of a second before he saw her shoulder jerk and watched her lose her footing.

"No! Damn it, Allie." He sprinted her way in a straight line as the sec-ond gunshot came just as quickly and hit the asphalt next to him. What the hell were they trying to do? Take out his kneecaps? Or finish her off?

James dove on top of her. She howled in pain, and the blood loss was immediate and profuse. Not good. "We need to move."

"James," she cried, but the rest of her words were lost in painful tears.

He wrapped an arm under her bloody chest. Allie's pain echoed in his ear. He lifted her up and took off. "You're okay, angel. You're okay." The chant didn't ring through with truthfulness to either one of them as he closed the final few feet to his car. "We're here. Easy. Stay with me."

Coated in her blood, James knew her welfare depended on how quickly he could stop the bleeding and get her to an operating table. He threw the front passenger door open and placed her inside. "Breathe through it. Breathe."

Her blood covered his hands, face, and chest, and the metallic smell permeated his nostrils as James jumped into his seat. The keys were in his pocket, and the keyless start recognized he was in the vehicle. He punched the Start button. The engine turned over as another shot missed by inches, ripping through the passenger window and destroying her headrest. "*Shit!* You're okay. We're on our way."

Allie groaned an unintelligible response as he slammed into gear. The few seconds it took for his car to pick up his phone's Bluetooth felt like decades. The signal connected. "Siri, call the office."

It rang twice before connecting with his private staff. "Afternoon, this is—"

"I'm coming in with a gunshot wound," he reported. "No paperwork on this one. Meet us at the ER entrance in—" God, too much time was going to pass. "Just wait until we get there. Prep an OR for surgery."

Having military and intelligence clients meant his team was familiar with certain protocols and lack thereof. They could move with beautiful efficiency, and he trusted them, but it had never before been personal.

"Angel, stick with me." As he drove, he tore his shirt off to use as a makeshift bandage and slow the blood loss. But attempting to tuck it around her while driving proved dangerous and futile. "Fuck!"

He didn't have time to waste by not driving, but she couldn't lose any more blood. James stopped the Range Rover on the side of the road.

"Change of plans," he told her, scouting for the shooter. Not that he had seen the gunman before. "I'm going to quickly bandage you and get going again."

"But..." Allie's eyelashes fluttered, and her coloring wasn't good.

"No one is behind us right now." Though they had probably already tracked his cell phone to find them. *Damn it.*

He fashioned his shirt around her shoulder and neck area, trying to tie it around her arm, ignoring her cries for him to stop, then used the seat belt to help keep it in place.

He leaned over and kissed her forehead then her lips. "Allie, angel. I promise you it will be okay. Can't die on me, okay, baby?"

"Mm-hmm."

"We have a dinner date then Turks and Caicos. I'm thinking you're pretty special, angel. Stick with me. Can you do that, hon?"

No answer, just her awful cries.

"*Allie.*"

"Turks and Caicos," she whispered, and it gutted him.

"Time to rock and roll." He slammed into drive and rolled his window down, ready to toss out his phone—but he didn't. If the CIA had tracked his location or where they were going, one more phone call wouldn't hurt. And it might save her. He swiped the phone, smearing blood on the screen.

The phone rang once before it was picked up.

"What's up, Doc?" Jared Westin asked in a kicked-back, gruffer-than-hell manner. "I heard you're causing—"

"CIA shot her." James ground his molars. "I'm calling in every favor I have with Titan. They know I'm bringing her in alive, and I want to keep her that way. *For good.* I need your help. Are we on the same page?"

"*Alive.* Whatever you need, Doc. You have my word you will make it to your hospital without problems, and the spooks won't be why she meets her maker."

"Thank you." He accelerated onto the highway. "And one more thing."

"Don't worry, Doc. I will take care of the troublemakers."

CHAPTER EIGHTEEN

ARRIVING AT THE HOSPITAL HAD been an out-of-body experience. Titan must have gone airborne to meet them. James didn't
recognize the faces, but Allie had an armored escort from his car to the
gurney, and the guards stayed with her as the hospital staff rushed her
away from him. He had a moment of hesitation. It would be easy enough
for an impostor to say they were Titan. But it would be dangerous too. If
the CIA ever impersonated Titan Group to get to a mark? There would be
an all-out battle within the paramilitary and security community.

With a prayer and a quick kiss, James let her go, knowing he loved her
and would see her in pre-op. She would make it. It would be okay. His
heart seized. He couldn't breathe. Because if she didn't make it, he would
have to live with himself having not told her he loved her when she was
coherent. But right now, he needed to cling to the optimism that she had
no choice but to make it through.

Quickly, he changed and washed her blood off then proceeded to pace
in a waiting room. Hundreds of his patients had walked this marathon,
but he'd never known the true depths of their hell.

"Dr. Tuska?"

His head shot up, catching sight of a nurse he'd known for years. Her
kind eyes were what had made him hire her. He'd thought her résumé
was impeccable, but her caring eyes were needed in situations like this.
Right now, they nearly brought him to tears with how reassuring and
concerned she was. "Yes?"

"She's prepped. Come say hi before she goes in."

The familiar hallways seemed foreign. The walk should've taken
moments, but he felt as though he trudged for miles before he finally
reached Allie's bedside.

Heart in his throat, James held her limp hand. "Your surgeons are the best, the ones I'd want opening me up." He had so much to say but didn't know the words. Tears were in his mind and his throat, though he wouldn't show them to her. "I'll be here when you get back. Piece of cake."

Her heavy cocktail of painkillers dulled her eyes. Her chapped lips parted, but at least she wasn't in anguish anymore. "James."

He leaned closer. "Relax. We'll talk when you're done."

Her head shook as though she were fighting time. "The... other... words. You need to know."

He had no idea what she was talking about. But whatever it was did not matter. She couldn't go into the surgery thinking that she wouldn't come out. She couldn't plan for contingencies.

The words.

She wanted to tell him the other words from the chalk writing she had memorized. Even at death's door, when she was fighting the most precarious of situations, Allie was focused on her project. And it would likely cause her more stress if he didn't hear her out before the surgery.

"If they come to you easily, angel, let's hear them. But then you have to go to sleep. We have to get you better. Do you understand?"

Her narcotic-dulled eyes lit as best they could. The flicker of a smile formed on her lips before she focused on mouthing the words. "Sic was smudged. No letter K, meaning incorrect."

"Sic, got it."

"Farr," she whispered. "Two Rs. Def was on another coil."

He typed into his phone, listening to her recount the words, what she thought they meant, where they were located in proximity to one another. As the last word came, her eyelashes fluttered shut.

"That's it, angel. Time for you to get some sleep." He motioned to the nurse who had been hovering by the door, and even as Allie's eyes fluttered open again, the anesthesiologist walked in behind the nurse. "Sleep tight. I will see you soon."

James watched his team of trusted friends work quickly. Then he stepped out of the room into an observation area.

More interested in Allie than he was the words, he continued to monitor the progress. Everything happened as it should. Minutes passed into hours until finally the OR surgeon turned up to the observation window and gave James a thumbs-up. He could take a breath.

When he did, the lead surgeon backed away, and James swept his phone's screen open, needing a distraction. He stared at the list of words that Allie had given him. Before, he had only taken notes, not processing. Now he did, and what stared back at him was a punch to the gut.

CHAPTER NINETEEN

TWO WORDS BUT ONE NAME, Dell Forester, stared back at James. He was the infamous former defense analyst on the run from the United States government—and who knew who else—for publishing classified information on his website, USLeaks.

The man had posted classified intelligence from various security agencies, hacked public officials, and issue advocates. Some of the information had been damaging to careers, while other times, it had been salacious. He'd exposed a powerful mega-star Hollywood affair and unfair equal pay contracts, while he had continued to post information from the likes of the CIA, DIA, the White House, and political organizations. Many times, his leaks had hit the news at the most inopportune times for those subjected to the focus of his limelight. It'd been obvious that Forester was playing sides and had favorites.

There was a national manhunt—both to catch him and likely protect him. Perhaps there wasn't a living person more controversial, *more hunted* than Dell Forester at the moment.

James rubbed his chest as scenarios fought to fall into place. He didn't want to start guessing until he had more puzzle pieces than the CIA trying to kill Allie and her running around with Dell's name.

Allie's list would be the answer. James dropped his gaze, and the other words taunted him with a familiarity he couldn't place—Farr and Stockland. Nothing that special, but next to one another, they scratched a memory, like a name he should have recognized.

"Hey, Siri. What is Farr Stockland?"

"I'm on it. Okay, I found this on the web for 'what is Farr Stockland.'"

The top two hits were for a political investigative journalist based in New Hampshire.

James's pulse raced. His senses tingled, and he switched screens, dialing

Beth. The phone rang once before she picked up.

"Beth—"

"I'm sorry. I don't know what's going on. Nothing is like I understand; you must believe me. But—"

"I don't care right now. Where was she found?"

"What?" Beth asked.

"When she fell. Where did you guys find her?"

"I don't know."

"Find out, Beth. Call me back."

"Doc, no one is going to tell me that. It's need to know. I don't."

"You do now. Find out," James ordered.

"Doc—"

"Find out!"

"*James*, I'm telling you—"

"What I'm telling you, *Beth*, is you have no idea what shithole you stepped in. It's not because she's mine. The little that I've figured out on my own says your team is working something questionable."

"Questionable is what we do."

"I need an answer," James growled. "Do the right thing."

He hung up and stared as he tried to understand the connection between a man who was leaking classified information, the CIA, an investigative political reporter, and a CIA operative who was being hunted. "This is big…"

Had Allie been searching for Dell Forester? Had she found him? Or maybe the people protecting him? It sounded like a reach, but not as absurd as what he was about to do.

Google easily located the reporter's name and publicly available contact information. A minute later, James let his finger hover over the send button of an email with his unlisted cell phone number and "Dell Forester" in the subject line.

Send.

What good would that do? Who knew? Maybe James needed sleep, a meal, and fresh perspective.

He stood up and stretched. Allie would be in recovery for—

His phone rang. Number unknown. The reporter? Or maybe the CIA was pissed that he had sent such an email.

He would never know if he didn't answer. "Hello?"

"Who is this?"

James paced the quiet observation room, trying to get his thoughts in order. He was going to come off as a nutjob, but fuck it. "Is this Farr Stockland?"

"Yes. Who is this?" the reporter shot back.

Damn... the email worked. "I'm a doctor outside Washington, DC. James Tuska."

"And? Your email was labeled about Dell Forester."

The truth seemed the best course of action. "I was just shot at, and my girlfriend is in surgery."

A pause hung on the phone. "And?"

"The last thing she told me before she went under anesthesia was your name and his."

"Again, and?"

"I've already said too much, and I'm sure someone is listening."

"Who's your girlfriend?" he asked cautiously.

James laughed at the million-dollar question. "Truthfully, I have no idea."

Farr chuckled too. "Well, I don't know if I can help you."

James's phone beeped with a text message.

BETH: SHE FELL IN NEW HAMPSHIRE. BEST I CAN DO.

The connections were just too close. "But I can tell you that she was in New Hampshire a few weeks ago, fell from somewhere, and—"

"Fell, how?"

"I don't know."

"Tripped or... like, jumped out a window?" Farr asked hesitantly.

"She's recovering from a brain injury. More than a stumble."

"I found a window in my bedroom... tampered with. It should've been locked but wasn't. Someone had gone through my home office while I was out of town. But we came home early."

Allie had been caught at the reporter's house and went out a window? James couldn't picture her jumping headfirst.

"Look, I'm in DC now." Farr cleared his throat. "Coffee?"

James walked to the observation window and stared down. The final steps of her closing sutures were underway, and the doctors were monitoring her vitals. Her bruising had been on the back of her head. He remembered her pointing out that her hands had been hurt and her fingernails were damaged. Had she hung out the window before falling? "I can be there in an hour."

After a quick exchange of vague meeting locations, James borrowed a car and phone from a doctor friend who wouldn't ask many questions. He ducked out of the garage and dialed a memorized number.

"Yeah?" Jared grumbled after the first ring.

"I'm leaving the hospital. Make sure they don't kill her."

"Already on it. What else?"

James rubbed his face. He didn't know. "What's Parker up to today? Can I borrow your tech genius?"

"He's available... but—"

He pinched the bridge of his nose. "Have him find me. I think you need to know what I'm about to know. It's more than I want to deal with, and you'll know how to handle it."

Jared cursed a string, and James could picture his friend shaking his head. "What the hell have you gotten yourself into, Doc?"

"It all started with a woman," James mumbled, and that was the only thing keeping him sane. "So long as she's safe and sound. But if this is what I think it is, loop her in on the credit for taking down bastard traitors." He seethed as he hustled down the stairwell and into the parking garage, heading to a car no one would expect him in.

"You know we're not in it for the glory," Titan's boss man said.

"Known you long enough to know that." James unlocked the car and slid into the driver's seat. "I'll see Parker soon."

CHAPTER TWENTY

F ARR STOCKLAND WAS ROLLING A large coffee cup between his hands when James walked into the coffee shop's door on the corner of Penn and Third in Southeast DC. He was the spitting image of his head-shot, which struck James as odd because that never seemed to happen. It also struck him as something that would make Farr more trustworthy.

Once eye contact was made, Farr stood up and greeted him with a nod. After an uncomfortable hello, they both sat down, and neither one of them offered another word. James didn't know how to broach the conversation without black-and-white facts, of which he had none.

"I'm a doctor," he offered. That was black and white. "That's about the only certain truth I have for you."

Farr nodded. "Everything is off the record."

"When you say that, do you really mean it?"

The journalist's eyes narrowed. "I do."

The coffee shop door opened again, and Parker strolled in, letting his gaze catch James's as he moved forward. Titan's guy would let the doc make the call on when to bring him in. "Have you heard of Titan Group?"

Again, Farr nodded. "I have. Legit organization."

"Agreed. I also called them. I'd like to talk to both of you. See, Titan is protecting my... girlfriend." That word seemed grossly inadequate for what Allie was to him. "I contract specialized medical services for secu-rity firms, government agencies—*intelligence agencies*—and recently, I met a woman who had amnesia."

Farr took a long sip of his coffee.

"It's my understanding that she hit her head in New Hampshire. Though she doesn't even know that. See"—James swallowed a knot in his throat—"I just learned where her accident took place, and she's in surgery, as she was shot hours ago."

"You mentioned surgery and that you were shot at." Farr's color paled. "Do you know by who?"

"Guess." James wasn't typically sarcastic, but falling into this mess had made him acerbic.

"You can't tell me?"

"I'm not sure that I can," James answered honestly, letting go of his acrimony and focusing on his mission. He rubbed his temples. "Because I believe that I'm walking the fine line between knowing classified information and seeing its fallout. I don't want to end up in prison, but... if I'm right, something has to be done. Are you trying to find Dell Forester?"

Farr didn't respond.

James chewed his bottom lip. "Do you think you know where he is?"

Still, Farr remained tight lipped.

"And who is protecting him?" James pushed. "Surely you have theories."

Nothing from the journalist.

Frustrated, James turned and nodded toward Parker, who had nonchalantly taken a seat nearby. Wordlessly, Titan's IT guru joined them.

Parker briefly introduced himself and sat down then turned to James. "Allie is doing great. Thought you'd like an update."

Farr rubbed his chin and then tapped his notebook. "This is what I know..."

Was it what Allie had been after? What she'd be willing to die for?

"There are five people connected to the current administration that have reaped the benefits of Dell Forester, more so than others." Farr rolled his cup between his hands. "Simply by sorting the information released, scoring it as a hit piece for or against someone, you can tally it."

James and Parker agreed, nodding.

Farr continued. "Michael Cobin—"

"The secretary of defense?" James asked.

"As well as the vice president, and..."

But James was lost in thought. Sic was on Allie's list, though she'd thought it was smudged. Could it have been *Sec*?

Farr took a sip of his coffee. "SecDef is in distant last place, but he's still very far ahead of the next on the list, so I kept him. That and his travel were curious."

"Why curious?" Parker asked.

"I cover the political beat, so the secretary of defense's travel wouldn't pop to me. But it irritated the guys who covered him. His connecting flights never made sense. Los Angeles isn't a normal hub. And when you're that guy, taking nondirect flights doesn't make sense. His press pool noticed. They talked; word spread."

Parker rubbed his chin. "What'd they come up with?"

Farr shook his head. "Nothing other than a suspected affair. Something along those lines."

"Huh." Parker looked at James.

Maybe James had the last key to the puzzle. He pulled out his phone and shared the notes screen. "I thought we had 'sic' and 'def,' or maybe it was '*sec*.' Other than those two, these are words from Allie that we can't figure out."

They sat in contemplation, before all shook their heads, unknowing.

Parker pulled a small computer from his bag and set it on the table. "Let's figure it out."

Both James and Farr stared at him expectantly.

"Go get a refill or a muffin. If this is something of the magnitude you two are talking about, and we have no idea what, I'm going to need a while." Parker's eyes dropped. "An hour or two."

Shit. James wanted to be by Allie's side when she woke up in post-op. But in the grand scheme of things, she would understand. This was more important.

Two muffins and a large black coffee later, James tossed a wrapper in the trash and took his seat. Parker's fingers froze on the keyboard. Farr looked up from his phone. Neither of them said a word as they watched Parker process whatever was on the screen.

Seconds trickled by until he whispered, "Found it."

"Really?" Farr asked.

With his eyebrows up, Parker nodded. "Yeah. And fuck, man. Allie did good. Even if she can't remember."

James searched Parker's face. "So…"

He grabbed a flimsy napkin and a marker from his bag then wrote out, "Dell's in LA. SecDef has him in a secure location." After James and Farr had read it, Parker took the napkin, shredded it, and dropped it into his hot coffee.

James's world wasn't politics, but he still felt the bottom of the world drop out. The secretary of defense of the United States of America was aiding and harboring an intelligence-leaking fugitive.

"And you figured this out how?" Farr asked, as if he were in a state of disbelief.

"Those are message board handles." Parker motioned to James, referencing the unknown words. "They connect to websites that have encrypted credit cards. The data that's stored on them is assigned to servers that process payments for various services. The SecDef used UberEats. Maybe to feed Forester? Maybe SecDef likes to have someone bring him a taco." Parker smirked. "It was paid for with prepaid debit cards, but those were purchased with cash from a withdrawal made from his ATM with one of his normal cards."

"Uh…" Farr's mouth remained open as James tried to follow what Parker had just said. "You did what?"

"I followed the money," Parker summarized. "Allie had the missing pieces of the puzzle."

"You figured this out by fast-food delivery?" Farr asked.

Parker lifted a shoulder. "FBI busted a money launderer in Russia once because he accidentally used an account to buy his wife flowers."

"And… those were the handles?" James asked. "How would she have had those?"

Parker's eyes narrowed, and his opinion was written all over his face. "They originated inside Langley."

Farr's jaw unhinged further, and James likely mirrored his expression. Allie had discovered a mole? "Why didn't they kill her?"

Parker shrugged. "Sometimes when they don't know what's out there, it's easier to keep someone alive."

Farr's head shot back and forth between them. "Who? Your girlfriend?"

But then the CIA figured out what she had known, or not, told others or not, and decided it was time to kill her? Was that why there was a change in orders? From not helping her recover to taking her out? But Beth said there wasn't—so a rogue team? A flipped agent?

Parker tilted his head toward James. "What do you want to do?"

"I trust Jared to handle this." He leaned back, exhausted by the magnitude of what Allie had been chasing. "And Farr—"

"When it's time," Farr cut in, "I'll be available."

"He can get the exclusive." Parker shut his laptop. "People and their agendas. Traitors and moles. They never learn, and they always lose."

CHAPTER TWENTY-ONE

Two Weeks Later

ALLIE'S STOMACH WAS IN HER throat as she chewed the inside of her mouth. But she refused to let any of her nerves show as they drove to the headquarters of the Titan group. "Have you been here before?" She shifted in the front passenger seat of James's new Range Rover. "This person is your friend, right? On top of the bigger-than-life asshole who knows how to hunt and destroy a traitorous SecDef and CIA section chief."

"Yes, an old friend."

"Because he has a prickliness to him that makes me uneasy," she added as James ran a hand over his five o'clock shadow then threw on his turn signal and eased into the driveway.

"I'll give you this." The SUV came to a stop, and he shifted into park. "Jared Westin has a tough exterior."

"I figured that out myself over the last two weeks. *Helping out* from a recovery bed sometimes felt like I was under interrogation myself."

His lips quirked. "He wants to help."

She studied James's eyes, trying to find comfort in the earnest stare locked onto her. "Help how?"

"Angel, let's learn what we can. *Maybe* there's good news to be had. In addition to what we already have." USLeaks was shut down. Dell Forester had been arrested, as had Michael Cobin and Daniel Yardman.

Like the truth? She toed so close to knowing her past with the unraveling of the USLeaks story that she could almost taste it. Allie's heartbeat picked up. "Should I get my hopes up?"

"Not too high. But if anyone can help, it might be Titan. I hope, for your sake, this meeting works out. But if not"—James shrugged—"it'll be okay."

"You put so much on the line for me." Allie squeezed his hand. "Thank you."

"I'm doing all of this for you, and I'd do it all over again. I love you, Allie."

"Really?" Loved her? How could he possibly feel like she did?

Her fingers knotted tighter around his. For all the fear and uncertainty she'd had since the moment she'd woken up weeks ago with amnesia, knowing that every line she'd been fed was a string of lies, she still had a sense that everything happened for a reason, even as she was overwhelmed by the idea that he loved her too. "I love you too, James."

A lighthearted chuckle brushed past his lips. "Glad we cleared up one mystery today."

"Ha-ha." She laughed too, letting go of some tension.

"Ready?" James turned off the ignition.

"Let's do this." They jumped out and shut the doors in tandem. He walked around the hood of the car and took her hand. Then they walked into the nondescript, yet somehow overwhelming, building that was the Titan Group.

"Here we go," he said.

"I love you, James," she said again as the front doors closed behind them. The building would either tell her the truth and set her free or trap her in this lie for the rest of her life.

CHAPTER TWENTY-TWO

OF ALL THE THINGS ALLIE had expected when she walked into the war room, it was not that Beth would be sitting next to Jared as if they were best friends. This didn't feel like an answer session, but rather an ambush.

Her eyes shot to James, and her walls went up. But James continued into the room, dragging her toward the waiting chairs as Jared and Beth stood.

Allie's emotions ricocheted. Her natural fight-or-flight reaction teetered with the need to either confront Beth or haul butt from Titan's headquarters. Running would be so much easier, but she would have no answers. Fighting would feel good but would be short lived.

James said hellos, as did Jared. But she could barely gurgle up a decent, polite "hi." Instead, she waited for Beth to say something. What was the point of introducing herself when everybody else in the room knew far more about Allie than she did?

Nervous and tight-lipped, she broke free of James's handhold and simply took a seat and looked at Jared. "Thank you for having me." She paused and tilted her head, finally connecting with Beth's eyes. "I hope to learn the truth."

Beth took her seat opposite Allie, while James sat down next to her. Jared remained standing, and he crossed his arms over his chest. She could see why James had warned her about him. His demeanor would have been scary if she'd had anything left to be scared of. His very presence seemed to growl. "Let's get down to it."

"Thank you," Allie said.

"Beth," he continued, shifting his stance so that he could look at both ladies. "Say what you need to say."

Allie's eyes dropped from Jared's omnipresence to Beth, who looked less like the socialite than she had ever seen. Gone were the perfect outfit, makeup, and styled hair. In their place was a fierce woman who wasn't necessarily waiting for permission from Jared but rather was genuinely interested in his opinion. Her respect for the man was apparent, just as James's was.

Allie found that interesting, given how different Beth and James seemed to be.

"*I'm sorry.*" Beth put her hands flat on the table. "I followed orders. That's what I do. It's what we all do. But the orders were wrong on this one, and I owe you an apology."

A gust of wind could have knocked Allie over for how shocked she was. For whatever she'd thought was going to come out of Beth's mouth, *that was not it.*

"Some operatives might disagree," Beth went on, "about apologizing for a job based on bad intel. They would rather ignore what happened and move forward. I can't ignore things in the past, so I choose to say... that sucks. I put you in a shitty position on purpose, and I'm sorry."

Allie didn't know what she would do in Beth's position. "You don't have to apologize. I just want to know who I was—*who I am.*"

James put a hand on her back. "You know who you are, angel. I think what you're asking is if Beth can fill in any blank spots of *what* you were."

"Yes," Allie agreed.

"Seems like a fair question." Jared pulled out a chair and sat down to face Beth. "The cleanup team destroyed all of Allie's personal items?"

"Sorry." Beth nodded. "There are things I can share. If you want to go back."

Jared rubbed his chin. "Here's the offer: If you want your old job, you talk to Beth, then after you leave here, somebody will find you. Everything will start back up again, and you'll be back on payroll. Or if you don't want to, it's all still okay. Beth will answer a few questions."

"It's that... simple?" Allie tried to understand how information she had fought so hard for was now readily available and apparently came with a job offer.

"Hardly." Jared laughed. "James, you ready for that coffee?"

James pushed back in his chair. "Military guys think they make better coffee than doctors. What kind of bullshit is that?"

Allie turned to James. "You're leaving?"

He shrugged. "I could stay, and Boss Man over there could regale you with stories of our time in Africa and the Eastern Bloc. Or he tells a hell of a Roman-and-Beth get-together story, but I'd recommend holding out until he's had a beer or two."

Jared chuckled. Beth partially hid a smirk.

James joined in the laugher. "That's when the Boss-Man-esque sage life advice starts to pour out."

Beth failed to hide a smile. Allie stared at them all, unsure that Jared could give life advice, and she didn't know what to think about James wanting to abandon her with Beth.

"Titan's kitchen," Jared said, "was recently redecorated as part of some environmentalist reality TV headache. I liked the people, not the cameras. Though we did get a top-of-the-line, push-one-button coffeemaker out of it."

James scowled. "Sounds deceptively complicated."

"One, we don't have to drink Rocco's military mud anymore, and two…" Jared lifted a shoulder. "That's about it. Rocco can't make the coffee anymore. One button."

"It's a Keurig." Beth rolled her eyes, teasing Jared. "The way they talk, you'd think they just landed a man on the moon again. It's great. They love it."

Allie laughed, softening to the banter.

"We love it." Jared pushed out of his chair. "Beth, brief Allie. Fill in the holes. Starting with her credentials. Read her in to her old files. The Agency is going to want her reacclimated quickly. Whatever you can do to help with that will be appreciated."

Allie broke out in a full-body shiver. *The Agency wants her…*

"And Allie?" Jared leveled his Boss Man stare at her, and she understood why James had issued all the warnings. It was as intimidating as it was supportive. "Now it's up to you."

"It is?"

"You have an apology from Beth. You and I will probably be seeing each other again, considering"—he tilted his head toward James—"he and I are friends, and you and he are… friends. You need to decide how you want to take the next step."

All the answers to her future were in this building. She knew it.

"Do you want to talk to James about it in private?" Jared asked. "Beth and I will step out. It's a big life decision."

"My options are I continue as a work-from-home Internet marketer…"
Or not. Adrenaline pumped into her blood vessels at the possibilities of her conversation with Beth.

"She knows which way she wants to go." James stood to leave with

Jared for coffee.

How was he so certain when doubt crept up on her so suddenly? The CIA had sold her down the river, written her off, and tried to kill her. She knew it all but wanted every last detail confirmed. And the job? Yes, please. "I'd like to talk to Beth alone."

James stood up and pressed a kiss to the top of her head. "Enjoy yourself."

When both men had left and the door clicked shut, Allie could hardly breathe for the anticipation.

"Welcome back to the CIA." Beth focused on Allie. "Your real name is… Corinne."

EPILOGUE

Two Years Later

"**G**ET CAT OUT OF THERE!" Corinne hung up her cell phone, tucked the knife's blade between her teeth, and hurried into the back room of a Titan safe house. And as their safe houses went, this one was *nice*.

Caterina Savage had no idea what she was about to walk into, and the woman was very pregnant. It wasn't so much that Corinne was worried for Cat; she was more worried that this wrong place, wrong time was about to get ugly. Her phone buzzed, and Corinne saw she wasn't the only one worried. The screen showed a text from Rocco. She swiped it open.

ROCCO: DID CAT JUST WALK IN???

Well, yeah, she did. This wasn't good. There was a reason the plan had been scripted the way it was. Corinne's phone rang, the screen display showing BETH. Oh, for God's sake. She swiped the screen to answer. "Hey—"

"Is that Cat—"

"*Yes.*" Was everyone in Titanlandia going off their meds today? Could no one just grab the woman and get her out of the danger zone? "Can you—"

"What are you going to do about it?" Beth snapped.

"What am I? *Beth*, get her yourself."

"Hey." Rocco popped back through the door. "Are you coming down already?"

"Get your wife," Corinne shot back.

"I've got it covered. James is on it."

"What?" Her head was going to explode. "Why's he here now?"

Rocco glanced at the serrated blade as she sheathed it onto her hip. "What are you doing, anyway?"

"I needed another box of..." She looked around, positive that Beth had said she put the "extras" bag up in the back room, which in this monstrosity of a house might as well have been three doors down.

"Point to the box. I'll get it. And the knife?"

Corinne gave him a side eye. "Why do people have knives?"

"To wound, maim, or kill. Which you look ready to do." He grabbed what looked like an out-of-place box. "This?"

"No, there's nothing back here that we need. I don't know where the other box is. Doesn't matter; let's go before Caterina figures out what's going on."

Rocco grinned. "Yes, ma'am."

They made their way toward where Corinne had last seen Caterina on the video feed. Thankfully, that was nowhere near the location of the surprise "sprinkle" party.

"Seriously, though? The knife?" Rocco asked again.

"I was cutting string for the balloons."

"With an eight-inch serrated blade?" He laughed. "Drop the Spooks and team up with Titan."

"Maybe one day." It was her standard answer. One that she'd considered more and more, especially as she saw Beth and Nicola enjoying the best of both worlds.

"There you are," Caterina said as she walked into the large living room opposite Corinne and Rocco. "We've been all over this house, looking for you two."

James stood behind Caterina, and the two men switched. Corinne tried to give them both a quick eyeball, signaling that they needed to get Caterina out of the house in a different direction.

"Hey. We were in the back somewhere. Planning this job is a huge headache. Thanks for your help."

"Sure, no problem." Cat's beautiful voice made the simplest words sound like fun. "I was just telling your man it'd be a shame to accidentally blow this place up."

Corinne could barely contain her grin. Cat didn't have any idea. "Which is why we're trying to make this op as safe as possible."

James and Rocco turned the wrong way. If they walked down that hall,

Caterina would walk into a room full of people still hanging balloons, and half of the guests hadn't even arrived. Mia hadn't even brought in the cake yet.

"*This way*, right?" Corinne said, trying to redirect the men.

Rocco charged forward. "No, I think it's this way."

"Hey." Corinne cleared her throat. "No, I don't know, guys." They were about to blow everything. "James, I think we're turned around."

He shook his head, missing every cue. If looks could kill, her fiancé would have been a dead guy. He was about to walk Cat into the surprise sprinkle *way too early*.

"He's got it, angel."

"This place reminds me of a place on Cribs," Rocco said, catching Cat's eye.

"*Ay Dios mio.*" She rolled her eyes. "Everything's a reality TV show."

Rocco put his arm over Cat's shoulders, turning them toward a sunken living room, and—

"Surprise!" Voices overwhelmed Corinne from all sides.

James wrapped his arms around her. "*Surprise* to you too."

"Wait. What?" Corinne blinked, staring at only half the decorations she recognized and a room full of people she loved. They were staring at both her and Caterina, and Cat seemed just as shocked as she did.

Two signs hung on the wall:

Happy Sprinkle, Rocco and Caterina!
Congrats on Baby #2!

It's a Wedding Shower! James and Corinne,
Get Ready to Say I Do!

"Um…" She turned to James. "Did you know about this?"

Corinne roughly translated the same words coming out of Cat's mouth to Rocco, but they were making out too much for her to catch most of the Spanish.

"I did, angel." James's eyes beamed. "And I wouldn't have it any other way."

ABOUT THE AUTHOR

CRISTIN HARBER IS A *NEW York Times* and *USA Today* bestselling romance author. She writes romantic suspense, military romance, new adult, and contemporary romance. Readers voted her onto as a Top Picks for Debut Romance Authors in 2013, and her debut Titan series was both a #1 romantic suspense and #1 military romance bestseller.

Connect with Cristin: Email | Facebook | Twitter | Instagram | Team Titan

Join the newsletter! Text TITAN to 66866 or click here to sign up for exclusive emails.

What to read next? Keep reading each exciting Titan World story! For more information, check out the books, authors, and websites below. There is no reading order, and each book can be read as a standalone in both authors' worlds.

TITAN WORLD SERIES:

TITLE: Flightpath
AUTHOR: Amber Addison

TITLE: Going Under
AUTHOR: Anna Bishop Barker

TITLE: Where I Belong
AUTHOR: Claudia Connor

TITLE: Bullets and Bluebonnets
AUTHOR: Jessie Lane

TITLE: Edge of Temptation
AUTHOR: Gennita Low

TITLE: Downtime
AUTHOR: Karyn Lawrence (aka Nikki Sloane)

TITLE: Target of Mine
AUTHOR: ML Buchman

TITLE: Never Mine
AUTHOR: Megan Mitcham

TITLE: Twisted Desire
AUTHOR: Sharon Kay

TITLE: Rescued Heart
AUTHOR: Tarina Deaton

Did you enjoy this Titan World stories?

Discover the series that inspired the World!

THE TITAN SERIES:
Book 1: Winters Heat
Book 1.5: Sweet Girl
Book 2: Garrison's Creed
Book 3: Westin's Chase
Book 4: Gambled
Book 5: Chased
Book 6: Savage Secrets
Book 7: Hart Attack
Book 7.5: Sweet One
Book 8: Black Dawn
Book 8.5: Live Wire
Book 9: Bishop's Queen
Book 10: Locke and Key

THE DELTA SERIES:
Book 1: Delta: Retribution
Book 2: Delta: Revenge

**THE DELTA NOVELLA IN
LILIANA HART'S MACKENZIE
FAMILY COLLECTION:**
Delta: Rescue

THE ONLY SERIES:
Book 1: Only for Him
Book 2: Only for Her
Book 3: Only for Us
Book 4: Only Forever

Each Titan and Delta book can be read as a standalone (except for Sweet Girl), but readers will likely best enjoy the series in order. The Only series must be read in order.

ACKNOWLEDGEMENTS

SIMPLY, THIS PROJECT COULD NOT have been pulled off without the talent of the authors in this world. Thank you to Jessie Lane, Karyn Lawrence/Nikki Sloane, Gennita Low, Amber Addison, Anna Bishop Barker, Megan Mitcham, Tarina Deaton, M. L. Buchman, Sharon Kay, and Claudia Connor. Words cannot express how much your professionalism, dedication, spirit, and spunk mean to me. For that, I will be forever in your debt.

Readers, this project is nothing without out. #TitanStrong. LYH (and if you don't know what that means, come over to Team Titan, and we'll tell you!)

A tremendous round of applause is due to the team that made this book shine! Especially to Red Adept for editing and proofing, All About the Edits for proofing, Hot Damn Designs for the cover design, and InkSlinger's Tara Gonzalez and Amber Noffke for getting the word out.

As for the Titan World project as a whole, again, another huge thank you to InkSlinger and also a tremendous thank you to Nicole Kuhn at N K Author Services for generating all of the excitement. Also, there are not enough kind words for Amy Atwell of Author EMS for her share of heavy lifting on this project. The woman is simply amazing.

To the authors that inspire and mentor me, those who know how much you mean to mean and maybe who I still need to tell: *thank you*.

Thank you to the retailers who are willing to try untested ideas. I won't name you but hope you know who you are.

Made in the USA
Lexington, KY
06 February 2017